Table Manners

And Other Stories

Susmita Bhattacharya

First published 2018 by Dahlia Publishing Ltd
6 Samphire Close Hamilton
Leicester LE5 1RW
ISBN 9780995634466

Some of the stories in this collection have appeared elsewhere, in a slightly different form:

'Comfort Food' in *Structo*, 'Growing Tomatoes' in *Planet, The Welsh Internationalist*, 'In the Lap of the Gods' in *Words for the Wild,* 'Letters Home' in *Rarebit – New Welsh Writing*, 'The Taste of Onion on His Tongue' in *Litro,* 'Dusk Over Atlantic Wharf' in *Tell Tales*, 'Table Manners' in *Beyond the Border*, 'That Face, Like a Harvest Moon' in *Lonely Crowd*, 'The Luxury of Quiet Contemplation' in *Lakeview Int. Journal*, 'Spider' in *Lonely Crowd*, 'A Holiday to Remember' in *Stories for Homes 2*, 'After She was Gone' in *The Bangalore Review*, 'Marked' in *The Lonely Crowd*, 'The Mango Season' in *Commuterlit*

Printed and bound by Grosvenor Group

A CIP catalogue record for this book is available from The British Library

For

S.B.

and my girls, Rohini and Mihika

CONTENTS

The Right Thing To Do

I push the cup towards Mrs Dalal. As usual, she is crying, caressing her bruised arm. She barely looks up at me but takes a deep sip of the tea. My Bhabhi tilts her head slightly, indicating me to leave. I go back to the kitchen, already worrying about the rice that needs to be cooked before Dolly and Rana come home from school. Then there's the fish to be cleaned and fried. And the clothes to be brought back freshly ironed from the istriwallah. The chapattis to be cooked. Why does Mrs Dalal turn up with her bruises at the most inconvenient of times?

Mr Dalal is a respectable man, a teacher in a respectable primary school. He goes to work on his blue Bajaj scooter, wearing the same coloured safari suit every day of the week. His moustache is impeccably trimmed and his shoes always reflect the sun. He hits his wife regularly. We all know that. But they are a respectable family, so we pretend we don't know that. And Mrs Dalal? She comes sobbing to my madam, my Bhabhi, each time showing off her bruises, showering abuses at her husband, and plotting to report him to the police. And after two cups of chai and biscuits, or on a lucky day, samosas, Mrs Dalal returns home, sated and at peace with the world again. Only to come back another day for the whole cycle to start again.

My Bhabhi is not like that at all. She is the queen of her castle. Sir treats her with a lot of respect. He never shouts when she returns home from her shopping sprees. I usually accompany her, to carry all those bags home, so I know how much she spends. Too much. (She sometimes spends more than my monthly salary on just one sari. But I don't mind, I also get big bonuses, not kicks and slaps like the maidservant across the landing from us.) Sir is never impatient when she takes hours to dress before they go out for dinner. He is kind and he looks into my eyes when he talks to me. He asks if my money has reached my old mother safely. I wonder why Mrs Dalal is Bhabhi's good friend. Why does she like to listen to her miserable stories? She needs to spend her time with some better people.

It's raining today. I see Mr Dalal in his khaki rubber raincoat, sloshing towards his scooter. The black clouds are hanging above the trees in the colony. The gulmohurs have cast a red carpet of petals in the compound. The petals swirl up in the wind and settle on car bonnets as though they have been offered in prayer to the cars. I don't want to go out on a day like this. I don't like the bottom of my salwar streaked with mud and rain, it takes ages of scrubbing to get it off. Mrs Dalal is hovering behind her curtains. I know she's waiting for him to ride out so she can come running here. I'm sure she has smelled the lamb kababs I've been cooking. Dolly has requested them for her after school snacks. Bhabhi lounges in the front room, reading Filmfare. She is going to the beauty parlour later for a full wax. She has the most beautiful fair skin. She needs to be tip-top for the dinner she's organised for Sir's boss tomorrow night.

Ah, here she is. The doorbell's just gone. When I open the door, I stare. This time he's gone too far. Even with the handkerchief covering her eye, I know a black eye when I see one. My mother had plenty in her time. Bhabhi swears out loud, and then pulls Mrs Dalal into the living room by her hand.

"This is too much," she mutters. "Why do you put up with it, Freni? The man is the devil incarnate."

I hover around, pretending to straighten the cushions, switch on the fan. I want to know.

"He is the devil," Mrs Dalal sobs. "But what can I do? If I leave him, where will I go? What will happen to my Kaevoo, maro baccha?"

I know that feeling. I know that excuse. I heard the same words from my mother's lips for years and years, before I ran away. I know the feeling of being helpless. And Mrs Dalal, respectable or not, is a helpless, pathetic woman.

I give her two helpings of kebabs and extra sugar in her tea. Her eye throbs purple and red, while she recounts the latest episode of Mr Dalal's tempers. I realise that even though Bhabhi listens to her ever so intently, she has never once shared her friend's trauma with her own husband. She never lets Mrs Dalal's sad life cast a shadow on their relationship. I am grateful for that. I'm happy that Bhabhi has a husband who respects and protects her. She is lucky. And I am lucky to gain employment in this peaceful house.

*

"Arjun's coming," Bhabhi exclaims, to no one in particular. She's reading her emails on the computer. She rushes into the kitchen, and rummages through the fridge. I stand back, watching possessively. The fridge is mine. She hardly ever opens it. And when she does, she puts everything back in the wrong place. She chucks out the mutton curry I made last night. And the chicken nuggets. "Finish these by tomorrow," she says. "Arjun's coming. He's vegetarian."

I am just as enthralled by her stories of Arjun as the children are. They call him Arjun Mama. And more importantly, he is an entemo– well, he studies insects. He does important research, Bhabhi says. She looks at her computer and says words like Milkweed Longhorn and Black Vine Weevil. What's so exciting about insects, I ask, and she gives me a look.

"He's a very important man. Make sure he is comfortable here."

I nod and go off. A man who studies insects is of no use to me. I have seen enough insects in my village, I could teach him a few names here and there. How to treat a scorpion bite? Now that's useful. Beetles are a waste of time.

Arjun Mama is here. He is anything but a Mama. He's like a film star. Long hair tied in a ponytail, smart beard, eyes that are laughing all the time. The children love him. He is very good with tongue-twisters and riddles. Dolly can't have enough of him. He is here for two weeks. Doing some research nearby at the National Park. With all the rubbish dumped in the so-called park, he's sure to find lots of insects. Ants and cockroaches mainly. What a job, I think, glad to be doing the cooking and cleaning for one house only.

He is Bhabhi's cousin. Her mother's sister's son. They grew up together in Nagpur. She has very fond memories of their childhood. There's a certain light in her eyes when she talks about those childhood days. It's always, remember we did this, remember we went there. Sir listens politely, but he doesn't say much. Arjun never stays in the room alone with him. He always gives a big loud laugh and runs to find the children. With Bhabhi chasing after him.

Even Mrs Dalal is not entertained this week. I send her back yet again with her bruised arm yellowing and her anger mounting.

"Tell your mistress to give me a ring when she has a minute of free time," she sniffs and strides off.

I shrug. Bhabhi has no free time now. She's busy tinkering with the 'apparatus' and 'log book'. She polishes the hand lens with her husband's chamois cloth. She's sorting the aerial nets and containers. They are going to find the Vindhyan Bob, she announces. A rare butterfly in Mumbai. In this concrete jungle, a rare butterfly exists, she giggles.

Arjun steps closer to her and speaks. "Yes, right in front of me now."

I see her eyes flicker and then she turns away.

*

They return home, tired and spent. No butterflies in containers. But flushed faces and secret smiles. I stay in the kitchen, avoiding them. I don't want to hear their laughing voices. I can only worry for Sir. He doesn't know. He's at work, working hard for this family. But she? When Sir comes home, later than usual, Arjun has already gone to bed. He claims a headache coming on. Bhabhi sits with Sir while he eats. She tells him her afternoon adventures in the National Park. Her efforts at trying to spot the butterfly. Her voice is too loud. Her voice is too bright. He listens, sometimes asking questions, scooping roti and aloo subzi into his mouth. I feel a sudden anger. I want to cook him his mutton curry. How dare this Arjun man make Sir have to eat vegetables all the time?

The days go by quickly. Bhabhi's moods have changed. She is now quiet and thoughtful. She doesn't accompany Arjun to the forests. He too seems subdued. He is all business now, typing into the laptop, no tongue-twisters or jokes. In the night, I am woken by the sound of crying. It is the sound of quiet sorrow. She's in the bathroom, in the dark. But I can hear her sighs. But why? I want to know. Isn't she happy with her husband? He is such a nice man. Her children are so good. Why run after that rogue? Her cousin? They have a history together, I can feel it. I'm sure Sir can feel it too. He is not dumb.

*

She finally lets Mrs Dalal in and listens to her complaints with rapt attention. Maybe this ritual helps her believe in her marriage. The atrocities of Mr Dalal help her to hold on to her husband and appreciate him. While they toy with their biscuits and tea, Arjun announces he's going on his last hunt for the Vindhyan Bob. Would she like to come? Bhabhi hesitates, glancing at Mrs Dalal. Then she shakes her head. Not this time, she says.

"Fine," Arjun replies. "She can come to help me. I need someone to carry my apparatus." He is pointing towards me.

"I would love to go," I say. "I've never been to the National Park ever."

They exchange looks. I stand there awkwardly. Mrs Dalal's eyes are popping with curiosity. I can see she is quite taken by Arjun's good looks. She smiles vacantly at him, her hands trying to cover the purple bruise on her arm.

As we get out of the lift, struggling with the apparatus, we hear a clatter of footsteps coming down the stairs.

"Wait," Bhabhi pants. "I'll come too. I managed to get rid of her."

*

I watch them together. They try hard to look disinterested. But I know a thing or two about body language. We struggle through the undergrowth, looking for this butterfly. Vindhyan Bob. What a name for a butterfly. I want to keep pace with them, but I keep getting distracted by everything around me. It is quiet here. Surprising as it is so close to the highway. I can see the tops of apartment blocks in the distance, above the trees. But it is like a jungle. There have been leopard attacks here recently. The city is spilling into the national park. Hutments dotting the greenery. So the animals have nowhere to go, and they attack the people. And then the people kill them. Who kill them in return. I shiver at the thought of a leopard pouncing on me. I look angrily at Arjun. It would all be his fault. Everything right now is his fault. I mentally wish we never find this butterfly. Will serve him right.

She gives a yell, and we rush to her.

"Is this it?" she asks eagerly. He brushes past me, and I smell the muskiness of his sweat. We look at the creature. It is the most ordinary of butterflies. Brown, speckled. No glorious patterns or colours. No drama. Just a common little butterfly.

"Such a boring thing this is," I say, already losing interest. My eyes flitter to the other flowers and bugs straying across our path.

He laughs as he swooshes his net onto the butterfly. "This one is a rare one, boring or not."

"Are you going to kill it?" Bhabhi asks. "Don't, please don't."

He glances at her and shakes his head. "I'm afraid I have to. In the name of research, I have to preserve it. Document it."

Bhabhi looks away. Her lips are trembling. "I didn't come here to kill the rare butterfly," she says. "Can't you take a photo? Let it enjoy its freedom."

But he has already snared it and closed the lid on the jar. The butterfly flutters, crashing into the glass walls.

"Let's go," he says.

We stumble back to the car. This time, Bhabhi sits in the back with me. On the front seat, the Vindhyan Bob keeps fluttering for dear life.

Back home, I rush to do my chores as usual. At the end of the day, I go to the bathroom to soak the dirty clothes in the bucket. That's when I look at the mug of toothbrushes by the sink. All these days, Arjun's red toothbrush has leaned shamelessly against Bhabhi's. But today, she has removed it and placed it in another tumbler by the window. I push the red toothbrush further away and grimace. It is the right thing to do.

Comfort Food

Li Xian cracked an egg and dropped it into the boiling soup. She stirred and it spread like a cobweb, clinging to the sides of the stew pot. The chicken was getting tender, and the pandan leaves left a sweet fragrance in the air. Li checked the rice on the other hob. Almost done. She smiled and looked at the time. Seven o'clock. The food would be ready in fifteen minutes. On Friday nights, her husband usually entertained business associates. It was the night she liked to spend by herself, reading, or just sitting by the window and watching the traffic and the city lights. She ate by herself, and always made her favourite dish, chicken rice.

The telephone rang in the living room and she clucked her tongue with irritation. Li did not want interference of any kind. The answering machine came on; it was her husband urging her to pick up the phone. He wanted her to meet him for dinner at the Crystal Jade. He had a crucial business dinner meeting with Mr Boon, the ship-owner. If he could convince the man to buy his company's ship, a promotion would surely be on the way. Mr Boon's wife would be there as well, Li was to give her company. And, if she wore that black chiffon dress, it would look very elegant.

Li took a deep breath and then exhaled. She couldn't say no to him. He had worked hard for this promotion, and it was close at hand. Her chicken rice would have to wait. She dressed with care. Her alabaster skin complemented the black chiffon perfectly. The jade bracelet added colour to her tone. She brushed her thick, black hair and added a hint of gloss to her lips. Simple yet stylish. She wondered what the ship-owner's wife would be like.

The Crystal Jade had pearly, ethereal lighting. Water reflections from the fish tanks rippled on the ceiling and walls. Paper lanterns and bamboo screens divided the restaurant into distinctive seating arrangements. The ashtrays on the tables were made of crystal; the napkin rings of bamboo and mother-of-pearl. A Feng-shui fountain bubbled in the centre of the room.

Teo Xian escorted his wife into the restaurant. His smile showed he approved of her dress and bearing. Mr Boon's wife had a gold tooth.

They were seated in a secluded area, beside the bay windows, and Li could see Singapore laid out in front of her. Beneath her feet, Orchard Road throbbed with Friday night intensity. She touched the cold windowpane, and she felt the vibration. The gold tooth glimmered as Mrs Boon made polite conversation. Li sipped her oolong tea and skimmed through the menu card. Her eyes looked over the page and at her husband. She saw perspiration gleam above his collar. He was talking a great deal more than normal.

Mr Boon rubbed his hands together and looked at her with oily eyes.

"Shall we order?" he boomed, and his wife's gold tooth flashed at him. A waiter stood poised with his handheld electronic pad. "Shall we start with dim sum?"

Plates of colourful starters lightened up the mood. Li smiled as she nibbled on her scallop dumplings. Teo helped Mrs Boon choose a dim sum to her liking. Fried Taro cake. Mr Boon stuffed bits of steamed spare ribs into his mouth between jokes and loud guffaws. Li asked Mrs Boon if she enjoyed cooking. Barbequed pork pies. Steamed chicken buns. Steamed octopus balls. They sampled and nibbled and washed it down with rice wine.

The second course was seafood tempura. Shrimp, calamari and octopus fritters fried in golden egg yolk. They dipped the fritters in tentsuyu sauce and remarked how delicious they were. How the delicateness of the seafood burst into exuberant flavour when dipped in the sharp sauce. Mrs Boon declared she made a better sauce because she knew exactly how much dashi to put into it. Li smiled politely. As if Li did not know how much dashi went into that. It was soup stock, after all. Whatever Mrs Boon claimed, she would never come close to cooking chicken rice like her.

The waiter hovered around, pan flute strains wafting above his head. The aquarium ripples reflected off his gelled hair. He cleared the table, and the hostess in a tight Chinese dress recommended they try the double-boiled shark's fin. Mr Boon's eyes bumped over her contours and said he'd eat whatever she offered. Teo settled for a crispy roast chicken and pickled turnips. Mrs Boon chose a lobster from the aquarium and wanted it steamed and accompanied with a black bean sauce. Mr Boon chose for Li. Sautéed Prawns with Eight Treasures in a Golden Nest. He said it was made to be eaten by a beautiful woman. Each vegetable represented a precious gem, like ruby, emerald … Mrs Boon changed her mind and ordered one for herself as well.

The conversation got round to business over dessert. Sampling the steamed lotus dumplings and durian ice-cream, they discussed if the ship was worth the 6.5 million dollars asking price. Mrs Boon declared her ice-cream was delicious. Li smiled and ate her dumpling.

The crowd on Orchard Road had lessened and the moon came up from behind the Mandarin Plaza. Li looked at her watch. It was close to midnight. Time to go home.

Mr Boon winked and said he'd be seeing them more often. Teo took it as a good sign. They opened their fortune cookies but didn't bother to read them. The two men stood up and shook hands. Mrs Boon's dress caught on the rosewood chair and snagged.

*

Li turned on the kitchen light and looked into the stew pot. The soup had congealed, and the chicken looked pallid under the fluorescent light. She told Teo not to wait up for her. She waited till he finished his nightly ablutions and retired to bed. She went to the bathroom and locked herself inside. She slipped out of her black chiffon and into her housecoat. There was a dried egg stain on it. She put her jade bracelet by the sink and washed her face.

Then she stuck her finger into her throat. She retched into the toilet. Her face contorted with pain and rage, the sound of Mr Boon's voice ringing in her ears. His leering eyes stripping down to her soul. The dim sum and the tempura mixed with the eight treasures and lotus dumplings—all an incongruous gruel—spurted out of her throat and sprayed the toilet bowl. As soon as she was cleansed of the night's intrusions, she rinsed her mouth and walked out of the bathroom.

Back in the kitchen, she put the gas on simmer and stirred the stew pot. She brought out her bowl and chopsticks and laid them on the table. The soup bubbled and the chicken took on a glazed look. She ladled the rice into her bowl and poured the steaming soup over it. A dash of soy sauce. She sat on the window sill with her legs up, the city sleeping beneath her feet. She sighed as she tucked into her meal.

Good Golly Miss Molly

"Rise and shine, rise and shine, rise and shine"

Mouli woke with a start. Her brain somersaulted from the depths of sleep to make sense of what she had heard. The sun's rays slanted in through the window, dust motes swirling patterns in the light. Outside the crows bickered in the mango tree. The neighbour's son revved his motorbike as the girls from St Agnes College giggled past. It all was part of an afternoon routine. Except that voice. Her dead husband was talking to her.

She clutched her sari to her breast, squinting in the brightness. The incessant whir of the fan disorientated her. His glasses were on the dresser as usual. And his watch. But he was never without his watch. And then, again:

"Good morning Miss Molly. Rise and shine, rise and shine, rise and shine"

Mouli turned and looked at Popat eyeing her cheekily from his cage. Popat usually did clever imitations of her, and often when the cleaning woman was mopping the floors.

"Sweep below the cupboards, no short cuts," making the poor woman jump. But he had never done an imitation of Satish before. He was gone a month now. So sudden. He had collapsed in the garden, plump mangoes had rolled off his hands into the ditch where the squirrels and crows feasted on them. She felt such anger that he never got to taste the first mango of that season, she did not bother harvesting them. She let the birds and neighbourhood urchins gorge on them. Even Popat did not get his share.

The parakeet looked at Mouli and jumped from one foot to the other. His claws clattered as he fluttered his wings. "Hello Miss Molly."

It was as if Satish was right beside her. He had always called her Miss Molly. There was a song, his favourite song, Good Golly Miss Molly. He'd tease her because when they married and she came to this house, forty-one years ago, she proclaimed to her surprised mother-in-law that she could not eat with her fingers. She had an Anglo-Indian ayah who taught her to eat the 'proper' way. And ever since, he sang that song under his breath as she tackled the fish bones with a knife and fork.

But soon she adjusted to the family ways. Eating with her fingers became natural to her, just as wearing vermillion on her forehead and praying for her husband's long life by fasting on Tuesdays. She was now the ideal good wife, but her nickname stuck. She would always be Miss Molly to him.

*

On their first anniversary, he bought her a parrot. She was disappointed. Her sister-in-law had been gifted a gold necklace by her husband, and she never forgot to mention it at any occasion. She laughed when she saw Mouli's present. "But Satish is like that only," she had said. "Always joking."

She turned her back to him as he slipped in beside her. Her sister-in-law's laughter still echoed in her mind. How could he do this to her? Why was he always teasing her in front of his family?

"Hey, Mouli," Satish whispered. "Are you upset with me?" He put his arm around her waist and laced his fingers with hers.

She nodded, not trusting her voice. A tear trickled down her cheek onto the pillow. She heard him laugh softly and then he pulled her closer. "Miss Molly," he whispered, kissing her hair. "Don't let them bother you. She's just jealous of you."

"Jealous?" Mouli said, trying to ignore his insistent hands. "She's jealous you gave me a parrot?"

"No, silly. Of this," he laughed and embraced her. "She doesn't know what she is missing."

Mouli turned to him, pressing her body to his, welcoming his love. Welcoming their first child into her womb.

*

Mouli got out of bed slowly. Any sudden or quick movements would make her head spin. Sometimes she saw stars, and everything blacked out for a second. The doctor said low blood pressure. She ignored it. This had happened to her ever since she could remember. She laid a finger on his glasses. She wiped them with the end of her sari and placed them inside a drawer. The children had left now. Gone back to their homes, to their lives. They wanted her to come with them, but she declined. They suggested putting the house up for sale. To have a developer build a multi-storied apartment block, where she could have a flat. Much more convenient. Safer.

She wanted to spend as much time here in their house, before it all disappeared. The mango tree, which Satish himself had planted as a child. Not deliberately planted, he had thrown his sucked- clean mango stone to the ground and gone off to play. A tree grew in its place. Home to new inhabitants and fruit for all to enjoy. It would all disappear very soon.

"Miss Molly how are you today? Good golly, Miss Molly," Popat called from behind.

Mouli turned around and smiled at him. "I'm fine, my darling, how are you?"

"Fine fine, I'm fine. Have you seen my glasses?"

Mouli laughed out loud. It was the first time since that day that she laughed. "I haven't seen your glasses, Mr Mitter. Look for them yourself."

She stopped. Popat blinked back and cocked his head to one side. Mouli shook her head and popped a chilli in the cage. She left the room. In the kitchen, she set herself to make a cup of tea. How tedious to make just the one cup. As the water danced in the vessel, she heard the neighbour's maid sweep their front yard. How much longer would they hold out? The city was mushrooming into tower blocks and concrete jungles. She'd miss the sound of the whispering trees, the crunch of the gravel, the song of the koel when the time came.

She pushed the morose thoughts out of her head and concentrated on making the tea. She remembered to bring just one cup out and the salty biscuits. He always had the sweet. She took the tea and biscuits to the verandah. It was still sultry, but she wanted to be out among the trees. Parrots screeched from the upper parts of the mango tree. She felt guilty whenever she heard them. What if Popat too wanted to be outdoors, free? Forty years in a cage was not a pleasant experience surely. Perhaps she should let him go. She heard him clattering in his cage. Then he cleared his voice, just like Satish did.

At the sound of that, her hands trembled. She set the saucer down, careful not to drop the tea. Tears came unbidden to her eyes. How she missed those sounds. His voice. His shuffling through the house, dropping biscuit crumbs and crumpled newspapers with half-done crosswords. She had come across a newspaper the other day, wedged behind the bed, and she had sat down and completed the crossword. Now she had all the time to finish them, one by one, before she was gone.

Popat called out to her. Miss Molly. Miss Molly. She ignored him. How did he suddenly begin to talk in Satish's voice? Was it a message from him? Mouli sat back in the wicker chair and pressed her fingers to her temples. Was this Popat's way of comforting her?

*

"Leave him alone, Shona," Mouli scolded her daughter. She was dangling a piece of guava in front of Popat's cage and making faces at him. The parrot squawked, scrabbling against his cage in an attempt to grab the fruit. "Don't tease him so. Would you like someone to dangle a chocolate in front of you, and not give it to you?"

Shona giggled and threw the guava in. "Where's my chocolate?" she asked. "Give me my chocolate now." She skipped around her mother, giggling and shouting, while her mother swatted her away.

"Chocolate now chocolate now chocolate now."

They stared at Popat, who seemed to be grinning at them.

"Arrey, this parrot talks," cried Mouli, delighted. Shona clapped her hands with glee. Mouli immediately called her husband at the office.

"I was waiting for the day you'd appreciate him over a gold necklace," he laughed. My heartiest congratulations to Popat!"

*

The phone rang. It was Shona. Asking, like every day, how she was. And how did it matter to her? Mouli thought bitterly. What could she do, sitting thousands of miles away in New Jersey? She rearranged her voice to a friendly tone and answered.

They talked for a while. Popat got restless and shouted at the top of his voice. Mouli stuck her head in and glared at him. She didn't want Shona to hear Popat.

"What's that, Ma? Who's there with you?"

"Oh, it's only your -" Mouli hesitated. "No one. There's no one here. Only Popat."

Lata dropped in later that evening. Her evening walks took her past Mouli's house. She usually dropped in for a chat. They had been new brides at the same time. They grew up sharing good times and bad, and lots of rivalry between them to keep their friendship interesting.

"You didn't come, Mouli," she panted, struggling to take off her canvas walking shoes. "Sarla was there today. She brought home-made samosas."

Mouli sighed and motioned her to sit down. She stepped into her bedroom to get the magazine she had borrowed from her.

"Lata is here," she whispered to Popat. "Fat as ever, still only talks about food. God knows why she bothers with her evening walks. She eats and eats all the time."

Popat chuckled. "Fatty fatty fat fat," he said.

"Shhhh," Mouli giggled. "She'll hear you. Remember once how you called her fatty and she heard you. She didn't talk to us for a month."

Popat bobbed his head. Mouli lowered her eyes. Satish had called Lata fatty, not this parrot. "I better get back to her," she whispered and rushed out of the room.

*

"Maaaa. Shona's let Popat out of the cage." Bablu screamed, running into the kitchen.

Popat flapped his wings and flew towards the open window. Shona wailed and flung herself on the floor. The cage door creaked, incriminating her. Mouli chased after the parrot, calling out endearments, holding out a chilli she had just been about to put in her curry. But Popat flew away. The children cried. Mouli comforted them. Perhaps it was for the best, Popat was with his family now. But that night, she cried in Satish's arms. The loss was so immense, it staggered her. She measured her happiness in the parrot's cheerful chatting. He accounted for every year of their wedded bliss. This is a bad omen, she kept saying. Satish stroked her hair and murmured comforting words in her ear.

"Who knew you'd compare me with a parrot," he said. "You once cried because he came into your life. And now you're crying because he is gone. Make up your mind, woman."

"Don't tease," she cried. "I feel like I've lost a child."

The next morning, she was woken up with screams and shouts again. But ecstatic ones this time. Popat was hopping on his cage, shouting "Good morning good morning good morning."

*

When the sun had set, and Mouli switched on the lights in her house, she watched Popat settle down to sleep. She draped a bedsheet over his cage and tip-toed out of the room.

"Goodnight Miss Molly," his voice came through the cage.

"Goodnight, Satish," she whispered. "I love you. Always have."

"I love you, Miss Molly. Love you love you love you."

Mouli was glad. She had said what she had never said to her husband in all those years. It was him, really. Wasn't it?

Tomorrow she would set him free. He could roam the skies and eat the mangoes himself. The tree he had accidentally planted all those years ago. Tomorrow he would taste the fruit. Then he would return to her. She was sure of it.

Growing Tomatoes

Hoda peered over the fence. Waheeda was in her garden, hanging out the clothes. The breeze billowed out Waheeda's kameez, making her look like a big, smiling balloon. Another reason for her appearance: the steadily growing middle. She glowed, sweetly pink, and this was her sixth. She waved at Hoda, her dimples deepening. Hoda smiled and turned back into her house.

It was time to get ready for her English class. Three days a week she trekked from her house in Splott to the language school. Most days she enjoyed the outing. She loved the smells along the way, of distant places, of other worlds. The aromas that escaped from the restaurants and kebab shops that lined the street allowed her to daydream about places away from here.

Waheeda's kitchen also wafted inviting smells, which reached Hoda's house. Sometimes she sent her food to sample. Biryani. Sheekh kebabs. Hoda enjoyed these, actually looked forward to them, as cooking made her homesick. She had come to Cardiff a year ago, second wife to Abdi Khaled. His first wife could not bear him children, and now she was too old. She lived nearby. Hoda had gone to seek her blessings. The wife, Fatma, did not look old. She had flawless skin and kohl darkened eyes. She did not seem to mind her husband had taken on another wife. She continued to stay in her marital home while Abdi rented a terraced house for his new wife.

Fatma sat regally on the settee and sipped black tea while she scrutinised young Hoda. She should fatten up, she advised. Bearing a child needed broad hips. The other women from the neighbourhood, who had come to see her nodded in agreement. No one mentioned that Abdi was too old for her. His passport recorded he was fifty, though he had said forty to her parents. It didn't matter to them, as he was to be their daughter's passport to Britain. To a better life.

Cardiff was nothing like Mogadishu. And yet, it was everything like it. It confused Hoda. It had the same activities of daily life. Husbands to please. Food to be cooked. Clothes to be washed. But everything here had a substitute, including husbands. They were called partners, ready meals and washing machines. Hoda did not trust any of them.

The women were of a different material as well. She stared at the white women. So white, so red, so loud. They shouted at their husbands. They drove their own cars. They wore their bodies with confidence. She could hear Linda yell on the other side of their terraced house. She heard the doors banging. She also heard other sounds that made her ears burn with embarrassment. Linda had four children. She had their names tattooed on her arms. Big fat bare arms that flashed their names proudly to anyone interested to see.

Hoda stayed secure within her hijab. No one could lay their eyes on her delicate frame. Except her old husband.

Was she disappointed when she had finally seen him on their wedding night? Terribly so. For some reason she had been imagining him to be like Dr Ahmed, who had treated her brother when he had been attacked the previous year. Dr Ahmed had fine greying hair on his temples, and a big, white smile. She had seen him through the curtains, but his image had stayed with her. Abdi was a big man. He did not have any grey hair. But his face was lined. He had a big potbelly and lots of gold rings. He had an agenda and that made her nervous.

Abdi needed a son before he was too old. He had a successful business, but who would respect a man with no heir? He was a failure. So a new wife was needed, and Hoda was the selected one. She had to fulfil her task before time ran out on her.

Attending the English class took her mind away from her hometown thousand miles away. She forgot about her craving for her mother's canjeero for breakfast. She was supposed to make it for her husband, but he preferred his first wife to cook his meals. Old habits die hard, he explained. They had been married for fifteen years.

There was a Polish woman, Martha in her class. She had been a nurse in Poznan. But here she worked in a factory, making cakes. She had to pass her English exam to be able to re-train as a nurse here. In the meantime, she stirred the batter for cakes in a factory situated on a street called

Memory Lane. Martha sat next to Hoda during lessons and never let her have a word in. She was in a desperate hurry to practise her English and get on with nursing. Hoda didn't mind. She was in no hurry to do anything except have a baby. But the baby was slow in coming.

The seasons changed the colours around her. It even snowed, an event that made Hoda shiver with excitement. But her shape did not change like Waheeda's. Fatma prepared all sorts of mixtures for her. Abdi filled her with multi-vitamins. Waheeda filled her with stories of all her births. It was spring now. The daffodils started to bloom. The parks were filled with such varieties of flowers, it amazed Hoda. One day Abdi took her for a walk to Roath Lake. Fatma was there too. It seemed to Hoda that she was walking with her parents, Abdi and Fatma walked ahead, comfortable in each other's company. Fatma was berating Abdi about something. Hoda lingered behind, wanting to lose them.

The swans huddled near the banks, tired of eating the bread the children had fed them all day. Paddle boats dotted the lake, young couples paddling away to keep afloat. Their laughter reached her. She wished she had a young man by her side. But that was such an evil thought, she bit her tongue. There were too many temptations in this country. She longed to go to the mosque, but Abdi wasn't interested. She must ask Waheeda. Abdi bought his wives ice-creams. That cheered Hoda up. She loved to buy ices with her sisters on their way back from school. But it made sense in

Mogadishu, so hot and sticky. Here, she was still in her winter coat, licking a chocolate cone. The contrasts made her smile.

So when shall we hear the good news, Fatma was asking Abdi, who grunted and looked accusingly at Hoda. She looked away. She spotted someone from her English class. A Pakistani girl. She was out with her husband. He was a young man. And they were holding hands.

Waheeda had been planting tomatoes in her garden. In five little tubs. Her children had sown the seeds, so each could have their own supply of tomatoes in the summer. The garden was filled with old bicycles, a small trampoline, plastic tubs and broken toys. Linda's on the other side had pretty much the same. Hoda's garden was empty. Perhaps she could grow some flowers there. Something to take care of. The idea cheered her up.

The visit to the doctor the other week had not been too good. The GP had suggested that Abdi do some tests. He had remained calm at the surgery, nodding and subservient. But when they returned home, he slapped Hoda. That ignorant doctor, he shouted. Insulting me. If you value your life, you better get pregnant soon. Your parents cheated me. I know that. Hoda cowered in the bedroom, wanting to escape. Wasn't it clear to him? Fatma and now her, unable to conceive? She remembered a poster in the toilet at the hospital where she had had to give a urine sample. It was printed in many languages, hers among them. If you are a victim of domestic abuse, put a green sticker on your sample and hand it to the nurse. Someone will help you.

It played on her mind all day. Was she a victim? But what could the government do? She'd be sent back home? Or sent to a shelter here? She had heard of such stories in her English class. Asylum seekers and their horror stories. She didn't want to be like that. Abdi was just frustrated. He was not interested in her most of the time. But now time was running out. And it was not her fault, she knew that.

Hoda bought seeds from the local supermarket. She could grow tomatoes like Waheeda. She cleared out a patch in the sunniest part of the garden and planted the seeds. She watered and watched over many weeks, but nothing happened. She complained to Waheeda, whose plants were growing sturdy. Waheeda clucked her tongue and laughed. She needed to grow the seeds in a warm place, preferably on the kitchen window. Once the seedlings came up she could then transplant them outside. Waheeda was at bursting point now. She grabbed Hoda's hand and placed it on her belly. The baby moved and Hoda squealed with surprise. They laughed and felt for the baby again.

The baby was born that night, a few weeks earlier than the due date. Now she was in a glass incubator, to be kept warm and safe until life took a hold on her. Hoda prayed non-stop for her. Fatma came to pray with her. She looked tired and old. Perhaps she knew Hoda's future. They prayed for the baby. They prayed for Hoda's unborn baby. Later Fatma prepared some porridge for Waheeda's children. The other Pakistani women took over from Fatma and cared for Waheeda's family. But they forgot about the tomato plants. For days they remained neglected, until one morning Hoda jumped up from her sleep wondering if they were dead. She peered over the fence. They had wilted; the leaves now papery dry. She rushed over and watered them, tears running down her cheeks.

Waheeda returned valiant with the baby nestling in her arms. There was a big party in her house. Women were sitting around Waheeda and the baby, singing Urdu songs. Allah be praised, she's a beautiful thing. How fair, how pink. She will get a good husband. The other children fought to get into their mother's arms. Waheeda shooed them away, smiling. This was the baby's moment now. She had survived the big test. Hoda touched her gently, remembering the fierce kicks she had felt a few weeks ago. Now the baby nuzzled close to her mother, no sign of aggression, only peace. If only she could be blessed in the same way. Hoda turned away.

On an impulse, Hoda skipped her class. She headed for the lake instead. It was a sunny afternoon. She walked around the lake, taking in the freshness and the colours around her. Children screamed and laughed from the play area. There was an excitement where the swans were resting. One of them had given birth. The mother covered her babies under her wings. People stood and watched and laughed. Babies spread love and happiness. She must remember to bring bread the next time she came here.

Hoda sat on a bench and watched the world. She had spoken to Abdi the night before. She had been calm, but firm. It was not an insult to his manhood. But could he get checked, please, as the future rested on that. There were ways to achieve what they were wanting, the doctor had said. But one had to start with a test. Abdi had listened, deflated. There was no aggression, just an understanding that he had known all along. But was perhaps waiting for a miracle. Seeing Waheeda's baby had achieved something. He was willing to do a test.

Hoda watched as the swan fussed around her new babies. The other swans indulged her. The mother was proud of her offspring. She craned her neck long and high and announced them to the world. The children came with bags of stale bread. But this time, the swan kept them at bay. No one could come close to her young.

Hoda watched her tomato plants grow. They were flowering now. Bright yellow flecks of sunshine in her garden. And one day, they were there, her tomatoes. Glittering red balls of sweet, sweet promise. She fussed over them, loving and proud. She turned back into the kitchen and got the cooking pot out. She was going to cook for Abdi, at last. And in her stew, she would use her home-grown tomatoes.

In the Lap of Gods

I met you at a Christian camp that summer. I went there, quite honestly, to find a prospective husband. These things happened in camps, I knew that. My best friend had met hers this way, and she was certain I would do too. But instead I found you.

The train whizzed past the smoky suburbs, the sunrise offered in soft focus through the Mumbai smog. The further we sped away from the city, the crisper the air became, until we were in the Ghats, with vast swathes of green rolling away from the railway tracks, waterfalls creating lacy tendrils on craggy rocks.

We sang *Jesus loves me, this I know, for the Bible tells me so* and clapped our hands. We snacked on banana chips and chikki. The other passengers joined in, their fingers beating the rhythm on their thighs, although they wore the markings of other religions on their bodies. We shared our food and swapped stories until we arrived at our destination. Our group of twenty, buzzing giddily with excitement, spilled out into the platform like bees homing in to nectar-heavy flowers.

*

And then, they introduce you to me. We are to share a room for the next three nights. We smile and say hello. Our room is a narrow sliver of floor between two thin walls. A bunk bed with a chest of drawers squeezed by the foot of the bed. The toilets and bathroom are at the end of the corridor, to be shared with ten other rooms, lined up like a stack of books. Each bed has a much-used pillow with a round, black stain smelling of coconut hair oil and a thin, scratchy blanket. Just looking at it makes my body itch.

You remove a shawl from your rucksack and place it on the bed. You pat it down firmly, making sure there are no creases anywhere.

"One must have a good night's sleep," you say, smiling at me. "At least this shawl smells of me and not some strange person smelling of oil and Margo soap."

I nod and look at my own bed. It never occurred to me to bring any bedding. Maybe I can use my towel as a bedsheet. You laugh, as if reading my thoughts.

"Your first time here?"

"Yes. My first time. But my best friend has been about two or three times already."

"Hmmm the Christian virgin then," you smirk.

"Yes, Christian and virgin. But not for long, I hope," I say, feeling brave.

"Which one do you want to lose first?" You are already putting your things away in the top drawer, leaving the bottom one for me.

I mean—well, to tell you a secret—I lean closer to you and smell apple spice in your hair.

But you finish the sentence before I do. "Looking for a husband?"

"How do you know?" Do I look so desperate that my intention is evident on my face?

"Most of the girls who come here do. Even the guys. Well, there are two specific groups—those who are here truly for God's purpose. That's about 2% of the crowd. The rest wouldn't mind hooking up with someone. And why not? Same mind-set. Same religion and all. Easier this way."

"And which group do you belong to? Are you looking for a husband too?" I ask.

"The first," you say, your eyes sparkling. "Not interested in the second."

But I don't believe you. You don't look like the people who have come here to be one with God. They have a certain aura about them. They wear crucifixes, and take God's name at every opportunity. They advertise their faith loudly, but your body is bare of any holy annotations.

The camp leader gathers us together in the compound and gives a welcome speech. He details out the activities and aims we need to achieve during the three-day camp. He puts us into groups. I scan the people in my group for an eligible man. There's one young fellow with a massive Adam's apple and a gold cross nestled underneath it. There's another one, quite overweight and with a loud laugh. There's you—grinning at my disappointment and whispering to me—"Don't worry. I'll sort you out!"

At the end of the day we sit next to each other at the long dining table, spooning rice and runny dal into our mouths.

And at last, in the quietness of the night, after giving up on sleep on the lumpy, smelly mattress, I move down to your bed and we talk.

I tell you how after a bad break up, my parents now insist on finding a man for me. I tell you how I have bought myself some time, to find Mr Right myself. I tell you I am bad at choosing the right person for myself. Both my relationships had been disasters. You tell me that you are not interested in getting married. You tell me you are studying to be a geologist. You tell me you will run away from home the day you get your admission to an American university. You tell me to do the same.

It's fun to share secret glances with you as the leader gives sermons on Christian brotherhood and the true meaning of love. There are testimonies every night. Young people who have found their true love: their Lord. No one else will do. They take to the podium and declare such experiences of love they have received from above. They cry as they speak, their bodies shivering with passion. There is only One Lord—and he is coming to save us all.

A girl with severe acid burns all over her face and arms cries as she tells us how the Lord accepted her when everyone else gave up on her. For months, when she was in coma, a constant light kept her company, and a voice calmed her and reassured her she was going to be okay. She had sinned. Her boyfriend had punished her. But now, she would be saved. She holds out her arms, her melted skin forming ridges and fault lines like the hills around us. But she is at peace, for she has learned that true beauty comes from within. She has found the meaning of life.

After dinner, yet again runny dal and rice, you produce a bottle of Old Monk. A quarter. We borrow tea cups from the kitchen, and drink it neat, the rum burning down our throats, making us giggle at our ungodly behaviour.

I slip under the sheets with you, balancing my cup and warm up against your hot skin. I smell your hair, which is reeking of smoke from the campfire last night. I tell you about my ex —a Hindu—who could not accept my faith. And my parents' ultimatum: to marry a boy of suitable religion and means before the end of the year.

You tell me you want to walk on beaches, and collect shells, and not care about anything else in the world. You tell me that your father, a master mariner, had sailed on all the oceans, and collected water from every one of them in slim homeopathy vials. The collection was preserved in a dusty showcase, the water long evaporated, and your dad no longer your hero. You say no one has ever understood you. What you want. What you need. You just go along with the flow, and feel the urge to walk along the sea.

I listen to your stories. Each like a fairy-tale, where you are the princess. But never in need of a prince. You tell me of the days you accompanied your father on voyages around the world. You and your mother fighting for his attention. And even now, you are fighting, you can never make peace with your parents. You have already walked along many beaches around the world.

How my heart stings with envy. I have only been to the local ones, with its offal and rubbish dredged up to the shores every day as offerings.

And then you turn and smile and me. The lamp behind your head makes a halo around you. Your frizzy hair softening its glow. I'm glad we met, you say.

And then, and then…

There is no one else in this world. My heart beats to the rhythm of the distance hoots of the owl. My fingers stray to caress your fingers, still tightly wound around the cup of rum. I smell the smoke in your hair, the rum on your breath and I am lost. I feel like time has been suspended. I feel a sense of recklessness, of sweet danger rushing in to envelope us. I'm not sure what I want but you are guiding me. You touch my lips with yours. Ever so softly it may not have touched even. I move forward, pressing firmly into your mouth. But you lean away. You give a little laugh.

"No," you say.

I laugh as well. But I climb out of the bed, unsure of my movements. You pull the blanket up to your neck and snuggle in.

"Tomorrow," you say. That's all you say. And then I turn off the light and face the wall.

The day has passed in a blur. As the evening mellows in, the songs of praise in the chapel crescendo into the night, challenging the calls of the roosting birds. The hills look careworn and patient, holding us in its cradle and indulging us. Sing, sing to the glory of god to your heart's content. There is no one here to hear you, except the birds, the craggy rock faces and the trees. The sense of being one with nature is overwhelming.

People around me are crying, tears streaming down their faces, lips trembling, voices soaring. I envy their belief. I envy their commitment. I glance at you from the corner of my eye, and am embarrassed to see you are looking at me. You have that smile on your face. The one that tells me there is trouble ahead. With a slight shake of your head, you motion me out into the open through the side door. We escape, running side by side, our slippers slapping against our soles, our giggles muffled inside our mouths. We stop at a distance, and the singing becomes one voice, echoing into the empty night.

We keep walking down the hill, taking in the smells: the raat ki rani, its intoxicating perfume mingled with the smells of cow dung and cut grass. We turn a corner, and before us is a bush, all aglow in the darkness.

"What's this?" I cry out.

The bush quivers with little pin points of light, sparks straying out and disappearing into the darkness.

"The burning bush," you say. "Can you just believe that?"

I nod but have no words to reply.

"You know, these hills are older than Moses. Older than mankind itself."

I look around me. The hills glow in the dark. Galaxies swirl above, the stars powdering the sky.

"The Ghats are older than the Himalayas. They're more than 150 million years old and go back to the time the earth had one big continent. We are witnessing something too old, so sacred that we must stop and pay attention to it. This is the abode of the Hindu gods. And when I look at this amazing geology, I believe in god's creation."

You walk towards the bush, and I follow you. There is no fire. Fireflies are nesting there. I have never seen fireflies before, and now I stare at them in wonder. They hover and they fizz, then they disappear. I reach out for your hand, and you hold it tight.

They have floated away and we stand there in the dark. I cling to your hand, and we embrace. The ancient mountains bear witness and I feel the shackles falling. I feel so light I could fly. I am not afraid to face my parents again. Actually, I'm not afraid to face myself. I look forward to returning home and being myself. I feel your fingers caress my arm, my desire for your touch increasing as we fall back on the cold, damp grass. I want to return to the real world with you by my side. Yes, that is what I want. But I'm too afraid to think about it. I suppose we will bury our secret here in the in the lap of the Gods, with our desires just fading into memory.

"Be like these ancient hills," you tell me. "Stay strong and independent. You do not need a man to complete you, believe me."

I believe you. I am so thankful to you for this reassurance. We return to the prayer hall. There is silence as everyone is bent over in contemplation and worship. We sit down, still holding hands, our lips move in prayer. And I thank God that I found you.

*

We did not meet again. You did run away to America. I tried to keep up with your news on social media. You graduated and I sent you my best wishes. I did not find Mr Right, but I didn't mind. I had found self-worth, and the courage to stand up to my parents. They could not stop me as I too moved away to another city and lived my life according to my terms. I broke a couple of hearts and revelled in my power to do so. Both times, I thought of you and how proud you would have been of me.

And then I saw the photos you were tagged into via a church friend. Your wedding photos. You proclaiming you had found the love of your life. I looked through your posts, your photos. It was there, for all to see. A traditional white wedding—how very original.

I closed my eyes. I did not want your truth to shatter the myth I had created in my mind to guide me through my life. I took one last look at your wedding photograph—you were not the person I knew all those years ago. I certainly wasn't the same person you had met all those years ago.

Finally, I unfriended you and returned to my work. This was not the time for reflection.

Letters Home

2nd January 2005

My dear Asma,

I reach Cardiff all safe and sound and start working also. The plane journey was terrible. Seat was so tiny and they didn't show nice Hindi film. Old flop film. Food was so-so. Cold rice and dal. Hard chana masala. Chicken like cricket ball.

I am in Cardiff now. By bus three hours from Heathrow. Sorry, by coach. Bus, coach all same things. When you come to U.K. you also learn many new English words like me. Muyazzumbhai waiting for me at bus-stop. But one thing not good about Cardiff. I find out immediately. It is raining raining all the time. Small small drops, like mist. Not like in Dhaka, big fat rain that fall like stones. And so cold, my bones feel like kulfi. I think I am inside a fridge. Muyazzambhai bring for me a big black coat. When I'm inside this coat, I like Cardiff once again!

I am sharing house with three men. Two Bengalis and one from Syria. We work in Muyazzumbhai's restaurant. It is big and famous restaurant fifteen minutes walk from the house. Royal Bengal Cuisine. But there is no Bengali food. Something called curry. All food here named curry this and curry that. I'm learning to make chicken tikka masala and doner kebabs. But I am assistant, so I'm not cooking. Just cutting and chopping. I go to English school in the morning. People from all countries. One Bengali lady in my class, but she very British. She not talking to me. My teacher, her name is Betty. Her hair more golden than your bangles.

You taking care of yourself. Soon you come here when baby is born.

Hassan.

My name is Hassan Sadikur. I come from Bangladesh. I live in Cardiff two months. I am married...

10th February 2005

Dear wife,

Happy New Year. Our house is very beautiful. In UK, it is called terraced house. Many many many houses stand in one line. Long queue. All looking same. One night I coming home and not finding my house. I standing on the road and looking. All same colour, same curtains, same doors. I getting very scared. I lost in this country, this long street with same houses. I ask lady in the street. But she more scared than me. She say something and run inside one house. Then I remember my house number and walk to my house.

Muyazzumbhai says UK is 5101 miles away from Dhaka. But every day I smell Bangladeshi cooking smell coming from next house and I close my eyes. Then Dhaka is very close by…

My wife's name is Asma Begum. She is 20 years old. She has long, black hair and black eyes. She wears pink sari and pink scarf. She cry because I go away to UK.

19th February 2005

Dear Asma,

Today strange thing happened. I was walking down street when I see footpath green in colour. I look close by and see small small pieces of glass. Full street covered. I stand and look. So pretty they look. Shining in the sun. Yesterday Wales winning rugby match against France. People going mad. I can see stadium from my house. Big stadium with big arms sticking out in the sky, like a monster spider. I can hear shouts and singing. Like how we can hear shouting from Dhanmondi Stadium when cricket match is on. People celebrating with beer all night. And they breaking bottles on the road. Maybe tradition like that. I don't know what's rugby, so I ask man from Somalia in class. He not knowing also and he live in UK four years. He saying it is all fighting on the field. So I watch on telly highlights. Too much dishum-dishum, little bit playing. I not understanding. Here no cricket on TV or on radio. Muyazzumbhai call Bangladesh every ten minutes to know score. He having too much money to spend.

Bye
Hassan

Would you like to give the order, sir? What would you like to drink? Mineral water, fizzy or still? Anything else? Thank you, sir, will that be all? Do come again, good-night.

5th March 2005

Dear Asma

How are you? I call you on Saturday. You go to Lucky telephone booth, 7 p.m. You take care of baby, okay? Do not feel sad. I tell you a new story now. Maybe you smile.

Customers in Royal B.C. like the food. Yesterday Rafiqmia made mistake and gave too hot too spicy food to gora man yesterday. His face turning red like beetroot and he coughing. He saying bad words to waiter from Syria, his name Ivan and throw curry on the floor. His friend laughing all the time. They both shouting loud and banging on table. They say they complain and close down restaurant. Muyazzumbhai gave free dinner to them, but when they go out, they wink and show finger and run. I not understanding these people. They go to pub and drink. Then they come for curry again, but man with beetroot face vomit on table. Muyazzumbhai call police. They run away and now we have to give policemen free curry. Take-away.

I have. You have. He has. She has. It has. They have. We have. I haven't. You haven't. He hasn't. They haven't. We haven't.

25th March 2005

Dear Asma,

I am so happy today. I had exams today. One teacher asked me questions. I can say all the answers, very easy like. Then I ask her questions. Her name is Sian. I say it is man's name in Bangladesh. I ask her to spell, but it is something else only. S-I-A-N. Shaan. I think nice name for boy, innit? I asked her if she is married. She said no. Then I make big mistake. I ask her if she has children. I bite my tongue. I'm sure fail now. She says yes, a boy. I bite my tongue again. She's not good lady. But man from Somalia say many women here not married and have children, He know this because he been here four years. When you come here, you not speak to such ladies. I tell her you have baby soon, insha-allah. That teacher very happy for me and she say, congratulations. I'm very proud man today. My Asma having baby soon.

Hassan

Baby-babies lady-ladies man-men woman-women child-children

Dear lovely wife,

I am happy you are in your mother's house. Tell your Ammi to make soup. I have tomato soup from tin. Okay taste. I buy from Tesco. You know, supermarket, very big shop. Big like football stadium. When I go there, I get nervous. So many things I see, I forget what to buy. I think of Rehana stores in Dhaka, I laugh. It is smaller than one aisle in Tesco. And Tesco not just one supermarket. Sainsbury, Asda, Lidl… more, more, more. My head go round and round when I see so many things. So much food. From where they come? From Kenya, Argentina, Spain, from far away. I want to eat muri, but cannot find in any of these supermarkets. I go to tiny Bangladeshi shop in Clare Road, and there I find my food. Muri, daal, ilish maach-frozen of course. But I hear you cannot eat fish anymore. Not liking smell? So now I will not eat ilish maach also. It is cheaper here than at home.

I buy some baby clothes. I know you will say bad luck to buy before baby comes, but what to do? Now special price, buy one get one free. I also bought nappies. Please send me your photo. Muyazzumbhai's daughter having baby also. She has photo of baby inside stomach. I cannot believe it. Then he showed me, and I think, this like E.T., that bhoot. He get very angry. What to do, better not to see what you not supposed to see. I only see my baby when he coming out, not like bhoot inside tummy.

Hassan

I'm sorry but I have a bit of a problem… I've afraid that… Please could I have my money back? … If you don't mind… Please can I exchange this for a larger size? …

1st June 2005

Dearest,

It was raining today and I went to a bus-stop. Here bus-stop has roof and bench to sit on. And bus come and go like trains in Dhaka—with a timetable. Many people sitting inside. All talking about rain. How hard is raining. They saying 'tipping it'. I look at sky and suddenly I laugh. I laugh and laugh, and people stare at me. I look at the rain and think, in Bangladesh when the roofs fly, we complain about the rain. Here umbrella fly and people complain.

But it is good here. At least umbrella fly. Big umbrella cost £2.99. There roof fly, cannot buy new roof. But don't worry, I send money to Abbajan for repair on roof. No more plastic sheet on top of kitchen roof.

I watch on TV, floods in England. Very bad situation. But everything so good, every person is getting bottled water from government and helicopter come to save people and their cats and dogs. I say what a great country. In Bangladesh, when floods come, we drink cholera water and fish out babies from the water with our hands. What a lucky country this… our son must grow up here.

Hassan

Mustafa is Somali. Asif is Pakistani. Maria is Polish. Hassan is Bangladeshi. Abdullah is Afghani. Li Jian is Korean. Nao is Japanese. Ahmed is Iraqi. Bahaar is Kurdish… the bombers are Muslim.

20th July, 2005

Dear Asma,

The bombers were Muslim. Just like that. What is their country? Doesn't matter. What is their language? Doesn't matter. They are Muslim—that matters. I know now all Muslims can be terrorists. I'm afraid to go out. The terrorists bombed the station in London on July 7th. Muyazzum-bhai was in London that day. And you know what? He never come back. He was terrorist? Or victim? How do we know, because he is Muslim? Now I walk the long street in shame. I'm not ever looking up. Some boys here, shout Bin Laden when I pass buy. They spit and laugh and run. I want to cry. Do I look like terrorist? I shave my beard and moustache. In school also, very quiet. People very scared.... Muslim people very quiet. Betty teacher look sad, but she try to make us smile. I say sorry to her. She started to cry. Her friend also, killed in train. She say 'senseless massacre'. She said 'insane people'. She said 'threat to mankind'. I cannot understand big words but I know they are bad words. I feel I am the terrorist who kill her friend. I will never go back to school again. But if I don't, they think I am terrorist and come to find me. I am not free man anymore.

Am I a bad man? I don't know. I have a wife who wore pink sari to airport and cried when I went. She is pregnant. So what? Bomber was assistant teacher in school and he had family. He was Muslim, like me. Am I a terrorist because I pray five times a day? I hide from the mirror. I am coward. I have no job now. Royal B.C. is closed. It is now Polish supermarket called Ziomek. Do I want my son to be in this country? Maybe not. Here supermarket is bigger than our railway station. He will never be hungry. But he will never be proud man, always ashamed.

I know on those trains bombed, there were English, Polish, Italian, Somali, Indian, Pakistani, Bangladeshi … and one terrorist with a bomb in his bag. Did he say 'good bye' to the passengers before he push the button? And in which language?

Goodbye, my dear

Hassan

Do widzenia. Ciao. Hywl. Nabadgelyo. Ma'a salama. Namaste. Khuda hafiz.

Buon Anniversario Amore Mio

Andy squinted as the glare of the afternoon sun bounced off the golden domes of the San Marco Basilica, blinding him momentarily. He turned to his wife, worried that she would get sun-burned, sitting alfresco in the piazza. The fuzz on her head was hardly protective. But Maya seemed oblivious to it as she stretched her legs out under the wrought iron table, her mouth shaped into a half-smile, her fingers beating time to the saxophone's bluesy notes.

She had said she wanted to be serenaded on a gondola, drink coffee in San Marco piazza, watching the world go by. Wander through the maze of Venetian streets. Pose for photos on the Accademia Bridge, in the exact light it was painted by Turner. Be tourists, the two of them, without a care in the world. Before the treatment was stopped. Before she moved to the hospice.

Looking at her face, soft and smooth—at last a positive outcome of the chemotherapy—he could feel nothing but love, an outpouring of such fierceness, that he found it difficult to breathe. She didn't look like she was dying, wearing that cheeky cotton dress with red lips printed all over it. Her skin had taken on a tan these couple of days and she had been particularly cheery and energetic. Hardly a role model for the terminally ill, he thought. She would never make it to those cancer adverts on the telly, in spite of her shaved head.

She had barely touched the coffee in front of her. It was just an excuse to sit close to the musicians. Her eyes flickered and then closed. He noticed then that most of her eyelashes had disappeared. One or two clung to the corners of her eyelids. This upset him more than when she began to lose her hair. She was dying, dear god, could she not at least get to keep her eyelashes? It made her look bare, more vulnerable. He was surprised how such a tiny detail could make such a difference.

"Put this on," he said, waving the large sailor hat towards her. "You'll regret it later."

"Uh-uh." She reached out and dumped the hat on her head. "There you go. Do you think I should have some more ice-cream? I'm so hot."

"Should we go now? You need to rest, you know." He said, clicking his tongue in exasperation. He knew she would ignore his advice. She wanted to make the most of this trip. Every moment of her life was going to be worth something from now on, she kept on saying. He gave in to that. Sure, he wanted to make every wish of hers come true. But what about him? What about his fucking last wish? Before she died? Did she ever ask him that?

His eyes darted away from her, afraid she would read his thoughts. They had warned him, those lovely, warm people at the support centre, what was to come. They had suggested that he seek counselling. Those people who understood everything, but did they? Did they?

"I'll get the ice-cream, darling. Just wait here for me."

"I'm going nowhere," Maya said. "At least not for now." She pulled the hat further down her face, covering her eyes. He did not know if she was smiling under the wide brim, making fun of him or if she was just avoiding him. He left her and walked into the shade of the Procuratie Vecchie, dodging the tourists with their selfie sticks and rucksacks. This was the third gelato of the day, but she had laughed and said, who gives a damn. She was not afraid to put on weight anymore. At last, she could eat as much as she liked, and not care about the consequences.

Andy watched her chat with the waiter, who was leaning forward to catch her words. He could see by the way she cupped her face in her hands and give that one-sided grin, that she was flirting. And the way the waiter smiled back at her, like they were the only two people in this overcrowded piazza. Andy saw her as the woman he had met twenty years ago—playful, funny, feisty. The woman he had secretly loved, and couldn't believe that one day would be his.

When the cancer came back a year ago, he had wondered if all those days of living the rough life, all those cigarettes and alcohol had finally caught up with her. Did it happen because of the linseed oil and turpentine she inhaled while painting? Those days of barely eating, nights of no sleeping? What about the drugs? He didn't like to acknowledge the drugs. What about stress? There was a theory that extreme stress could cause cancer. Was he at all responsible in any tiny way for her condition now? What could have triggered those rogue cells to multiply again?

He reached the front of the queue and ordered two vanilla gelatos. Then changed his mind. One vanilla and one pistachio, he hadn't tried that flavour before. Then he changed his mind again. He couldn't bear to think that Maya could not savour the food she ate, the metallic taste a constant in her mouth. Two vanillas. He worried the young woman scooping out the ice-creams would get irritated. But she only smiled and held out the cones for him. He reached into his pocket to pay, but she shook her head.

"From me," she said, nodding her head vigorously to elaborate her intention. "Is free, no charge."

"Oh no," he said, looking around, embarrassed. "Why would you do that? I'd like to pay, please."

She shook her head and pointed to Maya sitting in the sun. "I see you two yesterday. My treat, you would say that? Gustatevi i gelati. Buon Appetito."

"Thank you," he said, and then emptied his pocket of loose change into the ice-cream cup labelled 'tips'. He mopped his forehead with his shirt sleeve and reached out for the cones.

That was all he could do. He joined Maya again at their table. This time, the musicians were taking a break, and the noise from the crowds around engulfed them.

"This is hardly the romantic Venice you were expecting, I bet," Andy said.

"Beggars can't be choosers, you know," Maya licked the ice-cream and seemed satisfied. "It's why we are here as well—The Biennale. I just had to come and see it for myself.'

"Yes, I know that. It's alright, I suppose. Not for me though. The paintings in the Ca'Rezzonico I can appreciate. But those massive hands coming out of the canal, creeping up a building façade—I just don't get it."

Maya threw her head back and laughed. She always laughed when he complained about his lack of being able to appreciate art. Him being the outsider who didn't get it. There was always this other self, this Maya who maintained that distance from him, did not share with him that tiny bit of her. Always.

"I'm sorry, I didn't mean to but you always resist modern art. Why? It's open to interpretation. That's what I love about it." She smiled kindly at him, like a mother humouring her sullen child.

"That's okay," Andy concentrated on the gelato. It was not just The Biennale she wanted to experience. But he wasn't going to let that come between them again, not at this point of their lives. "We all have our own interests. I don't mind coming here with you. I know you always wanted to see Venice."

Maya nodded, thoughtfully. She wiped the corners of her mouth and looked towards the pigeons pecking away on the grounds of the piazza. "We never made it to Venice, Tom and I. Your mother died, and we had to come home."

"Yes, that was unfortunate." But it wasn't, and Andy had been ever grateful to his dead mother for being responsible in bringing Maya to him. "It would have all turned out very differently. For one thing, I wouldn't have been here to feed you ice-cream every hour, on the hour."

And just as he said this, the bells of the Campanile chimed across the square. They looked at each other and laughed.

"Talk about timing," she said. "You were always good at that."

He winced at that statement. It was he who had found that knot in her breast. He knew her body more intimately than she had ever done, the folds and the curves, the scars and the moles. She had always been careless about her body, pushing it to extremes—be it the addictions she imposed upon herself, or the long periods of neglect when she was working on a painting. It was he who had insisted on getting it checked. The oncologist had mentioned good timing as well. Any delay and it would have finished her the first time around.

"Do you remember that night we first met?" Maya asked him. He pushed the cup away and signed to the waiter to bring him another coffee.

He nodded and turned to look at the lagoon. The gondoliers leaned on their bargepoles, bobbing up and down in their boats, calling out to tourists. A woman struggled to get a wheelchair up the steep steps to the promenade.

"This city is no place for a disabled person, do you realise that? I would never have thought that, you know."

She held her gaze until Andy looked back at her and paused.

"Yes, that was good timing as well," he finally said. "How can I ever forget? Your first exhibition. That seems like a lifetime ago, now. Tom was there."

They sat quietly for some time. Andy avoided looking at her as she ate her ice-cream and sighed.

"I don't want to bring up the past, really, I don't. Especially not today," he said. "But I wish we could celebrate how we met. Make it romantic. I'm done with all this guilt." He sat straight up in his chair and squashed the remnants of the cone into the empty cup.

"Why do you feel guilty?" Maya asked. "It's not like it was entirely your own actions and decisions. I was the one cheating. I was looking for something else."

"He was my brother," Andy said. "Why do you never want to acknowledge that? You two were meant to be in Venice together, all those years ago. Not me. You and my brother."

"But that didn't happen. We happened, instead. Why don't you accept that?"

The waiter brought the coffee and placed it in front of him. Would they like to try some of their desserts perhaps? Some cannoli? Or zeppole? She turned to smile at him. I can't eat anything, she told him in Italian. But he can try, why not?

Again, he winced, listening to her speak so effortlessly. She had spent six months in Italy with Tom. Painting.

Picking fruits. Working in an olive farm. He had envied their carefree life together. While he had been swotting up to be able to afford the lifestyle he aspired for. The café was filling up, and he realised that if they didn't order anything more substantial, they'd have to move. So he asked for the cannoli.

"I wish we had met another way. Another time. But it didn't happen. And you literally saved my life." She touched her stomach lightly and lowered her eyes.

"That still gives me the creeps. Finding you passed out on the floor of the ante room. Everyone was too drunk or high to even notice you'd gone for ages."

"You were the only sober person around. I don't think I'd ever seen Tom sober. He was too high to even realise I was missing."

"I really don't know what you two were up to," Andy gave a slight laugh and shrugged his shoulders. "How could you have so much booze and weed, and survive?"

"It's all caught up with me now, see." Maya spread her hands out, to make her point. "I've done this to myself."

"No, I didn't mean it that way. You've stayed sober since we met," he added.

"Not with this cocktail of drugs and steroids racing up and down my veins," she laughed out loud, jutting out her arm to show him the purple and red veins, stained with the docetaxel drugs she was administered every chemotherapy session. "I'm on a bloody high the whole time."

"You and me have a history of visiting hospitals," she continued. "But never for the right reasons. I'm sorry."

"Don't be. Don't say things like that. You made a recovery, you did."

They watched a woman weaving through the crowds, coming towards them. There were others like her that they had noticed all over Venice. Dark faces covered in headscarves. Black eyes, old threadbare clothes. Some begged, while some offered roses to unsuspecting tourists, in the hope of receiving a few pennies.

The woman handed Maya a red rose. She hesitated to take it, but the woman pressed it into her hands. She pointed at her and then closed her palms together and looked skywards. "I pray," she said, crossing herself.

"It's too late for prayers now," Maya said, twirling the rose between her fingers. "Pray for him instead. He needs it."

"Really?" he said, under his breath. "I can't believe you just said that. That woman was looking for some change. Cash. Do you think she really wanted to pray for you?"

He felt around his pockets but then realised he'd given away all his change at the ice-cream shop. The woman backed away, unsure of what was being said. She removed another flower from the folds of her garment and tapped on a tourist's arm.

Maya brought the rose to her nose and inhaled. "There's no smell. But do you know the miracle of the San Marco Basilica? How Saint Mark's relics were found within a pillar inside the building? And the entire church filled with the most beautiful perfumed fragrance when it was discovered."

She placed it in the candle stand on their table and when the waiter appeared with the plate of cannoli, she held it out to him. "Una rosa per te."

"Grazie mia cara amica," He bowed and his hand reached up and touched his heart. Slowly, he backed away from their table, smiling at both.

Andy bit into the cannoli, the cream smearing across his lips, little shards of the pastry flecking down on his shirt front. He patted his lips with a paper serviette and started to eat again.

"We need to talk about the future, not the past. You know that, right?" she said.

He ignored her and continued to eat.

"I need to figure out how this will all end. I need to be in control this time."

He still did not say anything, but brushed the crumbs from his clothes. She slumped in her chair and began to fan herself with the hat. The shock of seeing her bald head made several tourists turn to look at her, and then look away in embarrassment.

"You've said that before," he said quietly. "When I took you to hospital that night. But you managed to live for twenty years afterwards. Imagine that."

"That was different. I was desperate to live. But now, I just can't take this anymore. Is this life? Day in and day out in hospitals. Needles poking me, chemicals killing my body.

All for what? It's spread to my bones. What's the point of it now?"

"Yes, I get all of that. I know you are tired. But is this your time to go? I can't let you go without a fight." He paused, and carefully wiped his mouth clean of the cream.

"I want you to be free of me, actually." She looked away, but he could see the tears filling her eyes. "I want you to have a life of your own. Without baggage."

"You know, that night, when they pumped the alcohol out of your system, I promised myself that I would take you away from Tom. Punish him for what he had done to you. Give you the life you wanted."

"So it was just revenge that made you give in to my advances? To spite your brother?"

"Possibly. But I did fall in love with you."

"This is our last chance to make things right," Maya sighed and fiddled with her sandal strap. "To talk about it. We always skirt around the issue, every bloody year. But there won't be another year, I'm afraid, to ignore what happened to Tom. We owe him that much."

"What happened to Tom?" Andy half got out of his chair, his heart thumping wildly at what she had just said. "You make me feel like it's my fault. I've had to live with this so far, and will do—all my life. It's not my fault Tom overdosed on our wedding day. It's not my fault he died. We will never know if it was suicide or just bad luck. He did what he did to himself. He had done it before, but there was no one to rescue him that last time. No one is to take the blame for it, certainly not me… nor you."

"I never suggested it was any of our faults. But it isn't right to cancel him from our lives. To not acknowledge what had happened. He was too far gone, anyway, and our getting together was the last straw."

"He was always in trouble, our Tom." Andy gave a snort of laughter and leaned back in his seat. "Our Tom, right. What a fine wedding present he gave us. He will always be the centre of attention on our anniversary."

"He was too far gone. It was something waiting to happen, and it did—that day. I don't think he planned it." Maya pressed her fingers to her temples and squeezed her eyes shut. Andy moved forward to touch her, but decided against it.

She shook her head and wiped her eyes with the back of her hand. The sun was beginning to drop, silhouetting the Campanile. The crowds were starting to dissipate, perhaps towards the Rialto Bridge and to the cafes and bars there. Perhaps back to their hotels. They watched the groups of people hurrying this way and that. The queue still snaking away from the bell tower. People wanting to take in the views from the top at sunset.

"Twenty years," Maya whispered. "Happy anniversary, love."

"Ha! Happy anniversary, indeed." Andy looked away. "I'll be the last man standing because I've been the good boy. The hero in your stories."

"Don't say that, Andy. It's just not fair."

"So what should I say?" He threw down some money on the table and stood up. "Let's go back, Maya. I'm really tired now. Tired of constantly smiling—for twenty years, but wishing for something else. Of trying to forget Tom, in order to enjoy our marriage."

"Would you do something with me?" she said. "We need to do it together."

He looked at her and shrugged. She took his arm as they walked towards the basilica. The pigeons hopped over their feet as they passed, not stopping to peck on the ground.

"Let's visit his grave when we go back home. Let's finally do this much for him."

He shuddered and nodded. He felt a wave of calm wash over him. Perhaps this was the right thing to do. The only thing to do—say goodbye to the ghosts—before it was too late.

"Come in here," she said, stepping into a cubicle selling souvenirs. She picked a rosary with a wooden cross. "For Tom," she said. "To place on his gravestone."

He smiled at the irony of that. She kissed the cross and placed the rosary around her neck.

As they slowly wandered towards the hotel, the pigeons took to the sky, circling around the domes of the basilica, and then back to the piazza. She linked her fingers through his.

"Happy anniversary, love," she said. "Buon anniversario, amore mio."

The Taste of Onion on his Tongue

Seven o'clock. As the sky deepens into shades of violet and I wait in anticipation. I take my place at the window and watch the people returning home. The street, usually so quiet in the afternoon, except for the pye-dogs that bark all day, has come alive with bicycles jangling, auto rickshaws dodging around cars and the blur of feet on the pavement. The exhaust fumes rise up to my window, and I peer through it, like a bride stealing glances from under her veil.

I have nowhere to go, so I don't have to return. The last time I went out, I cremated my husband, and returned to this empty flat. He left me when without a warning. Without showing me how to face this world. Without a son to care for me when he was gone. I am chained to this house by my inability to face the world. But I have got used to this. I cannot imagine how else I can live my life. My wardrobe of silk and chiffons saris has been devoured by moths and mites. I wear this excuse of widowhood: a scrap of white cloth wound around my body. My body, once ripe with promise, has withered. Now the odour of my own decay clings to me all the time.

So I wait by the window, and watch other people. Especially *him*. He lives with his wife in the building opposite mine. Our windows so close to each other, it is hard to ignore what goes on there. I stay in the dark and share their world.

They have been married ten years. He brought her as a bride to that house. I was there, with the other women, ululating, showering rice and smearing vermillion on her forehead, welcoming her into the marital world. I wished her luck, and teased her to keep the window shut that night.

"Now don't go waking us up in the middle of the night, will you?"

She had looked confused, while the older women chuckled and shot knowing glances at each other. And him? His ears had gone red. He looked at me through slits of his eyes, and then smiled at his bride with reassurance.

Last night he made love to her. I sat up in my bed, ears straining, spectacles on my nose, peering to see. The streetlamp made slanting patterns over their bed, and I watched the long shadows move on the wall. I felt an electric jolt. I gripped the sides of my bed and felt the tension in the pit of my stomach. His fingers, long like an artist's, stroked me and his nails, trimmed every Sunday, scratched and made white marks on my skin. She moaned, and I cried, "Shut up, you whore. Disturbing the neighbours with your shamelessness." He banged the window shut. And I was left alone, unfulfilled, cheated out of my pleasure.

He's here. He rides his scooter up onto the pavement and parks it by the main gate. I shuffle into the kitchen, and warm my dinner. The local dabba service brings me my food. If you can call it that—the same runny dal and rice, same subzi and salad. When my husband was alive, we ate mutton every Sunday and there were fresh vegetables from the market every day. But now, there is only so much I can do with my savings. I heat up the dal and rice, and pour them into a bowl. I slice an onion into four chunks and put it on a side plate. By this time, he is climbing up the five flights of stairs to his house.

Balancing the steaming bowl and sliced onions on the tray, I sit by the window again. He's removing his shirt. I clutch the opening of my dressing gown, smelling his sweat, my tongue outlining the sweat-circles on the armpits of his shirt. I taste the saltiness and close my eyes. He drops his clothes on the floor, and she picks them up after him. She has found something in his trouser pocket. She removes it and holds it up to inspect. A bottle. It is the same story once again. A man needs his drink; especially if he's married to a barren woman. Ten years and no signs of a child. Thirty years, and my seed refused to bear fruit: I remember it only too well. So what if my flesh turned on the desire, the inside was a dry wasted desert, where nothing could take on life. Those years sucked out our happiness. We made a charade of living together, knowing every single time the passion arose, there would be no result to those meaningless actions.

She is crying and shouting at him. I hear her stinging words. They are an echo of mine. But I know better now; I know he needs the alcohol to forget what he cannot have. He steps forward and slaps her. I flinch. Forgive me, forgive me. Words swirl around in my head. My voice becomes one with hers. Don't drink so much, I want to tell him. It will take you away too. Like it took him. She moves away from him, face buried in her hands, shaking convulsively.

He steps into the bathroom. Ten minutes. He's going to wear the blue pyjamas tonight. The white pair is hanging on the clothesline outside the window, flapping in the evening breeze, dancing and teasing me to come and join him on that line. He shakes the talcum powder on his back, his chest and under his arms. If only I could just reach out and touch his chest, and stroke it and bury my face in the white flecked fur on his chest. He combs his hair carefully, first patting it dry with a towel. His hair has thinned a bit more at the top. I want to run my fingers through and feel the moistness, and smell the coconut oil he always uses.

He looks at her. She is still sobbing, her thin shoulders heaving as she struggles to gulp in air. He wants to have his rum, but I know he has run out of Coca Cola. She has forgotten to replace it. He is shouting at her, and she is trembling. She has to buy them *now*. He throws the empty plastic bottles at her, and she ducks. She goes out of the house and I sigh with relief. At last, I have him to myself for a while. I chew my meal slowly, and watch him cut onions. He likes munching them with his drink. I wonder what his breath would be like if he made love tonight. Pungent, acidic, sharp. I crunch into my onion, and chew slowly, letting the sharpness trickle down my throat. In the night, when I hear them move, I can whisper his name, and feel his pungent breath on my face, and taste the onion on his tongue.

She has returned. But there's no Coca Cola. She's got Pepsi, and he's not happy. She doesn't know, that it matters a lot, having Coke and not Pepsi with the rum. I shake my head in resignation. She will never learn. He yells and she cowers. Why, you stupid woman, are you messing up my evening?

Then he looks straight through my window, and glares at me, as if he wants to turn me into stone. I tremble in the intensity of his gaze. I follow the movement of his lips.

"Crazy bitch," he mouths and slams the window shut.

Dusk Over Atlantic Wharf

"It's such a dull day. Let's do something exciting," Lata switched off the television and looked at Anuj. He was lying on the carpet, solving the Times crossword.

"What do you want to do?" he asked absently. "Twenty-one across… Strong and wiry copper arresting teacher in retirement."

"I don't know… let's go out for dinner or something." Lata's eyes brightened. A new Indian restaurant had opened in Mermaid's Quay. She had read the review in the Western Mail and it was not the usual chicken tikka and curry, but authentic recipes from the Malabar Coast.

"Only if we don't eat Balti," Anuj chewed on his pencil. "Want to try Welsh? The Armless Dragon is good. Had a meal there once with the department."

"No. There's food in the fridge." She walked to the window. The sky loomed large and grey over the chimney tops and television aerials. Lata missed the drama of colours played out in the sky. She observed it had been the same dull grey throughout the day. Just like those bed sheets back home—after they came back from the dhobi. Ma had been livid. She had screamed at the poor man, threatening never to give him linen to be washed again. Afraid of losing this job, the dhobi had promised to wash Ma's linen free of cost for a whole month.

Lata smiled at the memory and gazed out. She scanned the street, hoping to find some movement. Maybe catch a glimpse of the people who lived on her street. The narrow-terraced houses, huddled together, and looked at her with lacy eyes. They seemed to be observing her and whispering among themselves. These houses, with their translucent curtains, showed a promise of friendship, but not enough to let you see through them. Filled with strangers, not neighbours. She was too afraid to befriend them, not knowing if she would be welcomed, and not bothering to find out.

Hindu Colony, Lane One. She knew everyone who lived in her building, and many more that lived around. Evenings meant strolling down the shady lanes with friends, munching on hot, roasted peanuts, laughing and chatting. Not self-conscious, not out of place.

She looked at her husband still attacking the crossword; his forehead creased and pencil well chewed. She could finish it in forty minutes, but of course she wouldn't tell him that. He had been in Cardiff for six years before they got married, five years and eight months more than her. And he thought he was as British as the white people. Well, of course he was. He had the red passport, hadn't he? Wasn't that the reason Baba got her married to him? Good future for you, beti, he had said. How did Baba know? He had never stepped out of India ever. So did he not give Ma a good future? This poky little house on this draughty street, cold seeping into the bones. Cooking and cleaning, hoovering and washing… cleaning the toilet. My god. Yet, her father believed he had made the right choice for her. Good future for you, beti, his voice echoed and she gulped back her resentment.

Anuj looked up finally. "Finished it."

She gave him a quavering smile. "I like doing crosswords as well."

"Oh, then I must get another copy of the Times… or I'll Xerox it in office. Save money that way and paper too. You know, you shouldn't waste paper, should recycle and all that… did you do that in India?"

She did not reply.

"Now, you want to do something exciting," Anuj looked at her, concerned. "My bride is already bored? Look, the mehendi has not yet faded from your palms."

"Liar! Look, it's faded," Lata laughed, "I'm not a bride anymore!" She waved her hands about and did a mock pirouette in front of him.

Anuj burst out laughing. "You are quite funny, you know…"

"Yes, Mina used to say, you know Mina, my best friend back home, said I was the joker in the group. Stand-up comedian."

Anuj looked at her steadily, not smiling. He took her hands in his. "This is your home now. Cardiff is home. That is India, your parents' home. You must adjust as soon as you can, my dear. Otherwise things will be more difficult for you, isn't it?"

Lata stared at Anuj, and then at her hennaed hands. It was true, she was his bride and wanted to love him desperately, but he made it so difficult for her at times.

"Let's go to the Bay, and watch a movie," he said, pulling her close to him. Lata closed her eyes and held on to him, breathing in his scent. He smelled so clean, of that lovely shower gel she'd bought in Boots. She took a deep breath. She would learn to love him.

Yes, Ma had said so; she would learn to love him.

"Let's go watch a movie," she whispered.

They were lucky to find a parking space. Atlantic Wharf was packed with Saturday night revellers. Lata looked out of the window, while Anuj tried to squeeze their Ford between two king-size family cars. A gaggle of teenage girls stood outside the nightclub, talking in high-pitched voices. They wore tiny leather skirts and tank tops, and braced themselves against the biting cold by smoking and hugging themselves. They tottered on high heels that click clacked as they walked. Lata looked down at her blue silk sari and black overcoat. She felt like an old woman, even though this sari was what she had worn at her engagement party back home. As she watched the pony-tailed mascara blinded girls striding up and down the pavement, her clothes weighed her down. She looked at Anuj from the corner of her eye. He was busy locking the car, taking her hand, crossing the road. She sighed. Good, so these memsahibs had no effect on him.

She remembered her bother Bhushan, and his obsession with Jennifer Lopez. She could never enter his bedroom without feeling smothered by the posters on the wall. Those pictures of half-naked women made her feel very embarrassed. She would argue with him that if he admired those sorts of pictures, then he surely did not respect women. Bhushan would shrug and tell her that if Jennifer dressed the way she did, he'd lose respect for Jennifer.

Anuj guided her through the door into the leisure centre. Immediately they were enveloped in an inviting, warm blanket of aromas. Coffee and spices smelled so good together, Lata inhaled deeply and smiled. The bars were packed, and long queues snaked in front of the restaurants.

"You wait here, I'll get the tickets." Anuj deposited her in a corner and left.

There were people everywhere. Lata watched the crowd in delight. Families were out, holding hands, their faces shining. Lovers, oblivious to their surrounding were laughing, touching and kissing. Children ran about, screaming, chasing each other. They are lovely, she thought, soaking in their happiness. Those girls there, just like Mina and me, skipping college to watch a film. What a day that was! Slinking out of class and running at top speed towards the bus-stop, laughing all the way. Mina got hiccups and she had them all the way to the theatre. And that day, we caught Bhushan, out with his girlfriend. I blackmailed him into taking those disgusting posters off the wall. She laughed out loud at the memory and a man standing next to her exclaimed, "You alright, love?"

His breath smelled sharp. He leaned towards her till she could see the sparkle in his eyes. Lata shrank back. Words jumbled in her mouth. He winked at her and disappeared in the crowd. Lata trembled. Was that man trying to flirt with her? She couldn't even answer him. Her English was good, but she couldn't follow his accent very well, and it made her conscious of her own.

"You alright, my dear?"

Lata jumped. It was Anuj. "What is the answer to that?" she asked.

"Answer to what?"

"Why do people here ask, 'you alright?' Nothing is visibly wrong with me, is there?"

"What are you talking about? Come on now, I have a treat for you." His eyebrows were furrowed and his lips were set to a thin line.

"Are you alright?" she asked.

"Yeah." He looked baffled. Then he smiled and pinched her cheek. "We're watching a Bollywood film." He said and handed her the tickets with a flourish. "Happy, darling?"

Lata hugged his arm and laughed. "That's a great movie. It's a hit back in India."

"Let me buy some popcorn. You wait here." Lata stood behind the ticket counter and looked up at the monitor displaying the movies being showed that night. All the

English films were sold out. Could that be the reason why he bought the Hindi film tickets? Lata looked at Anuj in the distance, paying for the popcorn. He was smiling at the man behind the counter. No, he really did want to watch this film with me, she decided.

"Lata, you– are you okay? Your cheeks are flushed." Anuj was back, balancing two jumbo popcorns and a cola.

"No, no, I'm fine. I'm all excited. I'm alright." They looked at each other and laughed nervously.

In the darkened theatre, Anuj finished most of the popcorn. He thought the music was too loud, but the action was up to Hollywood standard. Lata stared greedily at the screen, her eyes devouring the background images of her hometown, where the film had been shot.

"There's Marine Drive, oh look, my college. See the beach? That's where we used to go after class. You get amazing ice-cream there. That's Shivaji Park. It's very close to our house. I'll take you there when we go back to visit. Only a twenty minute walk, but we can take a cab… Bhushan jogs there, you know. That's his girlfriend's house…"

"Shhh, watch the movie. Don't give running commentary to the other people. It's bad manners." Anuj sank deeper into his seat. He took her hand in his, but she was too engrossed to take notice. If only the actor would move aside, she would see Churchgate station in the distance. Lata savoured every moment of the film. She didn't pay attention to the storyline, she but relived her own life as it used to be in those places that flashed across the screen.

"Aaah, look! Jogger's Park. Look at the sea, Anuj, isn't it amazing? The sunset looks awesome."

"Yeah, it's beautiful," he whispered back, squeezing her hand. "Now watch the film, not the background."

They walked out of the theatre, bright eyed and tired. Lata was happy, having spent three hours in sunny Mumbai, reliving her past.

"We must buy a DVD player," she told Anuj. "I can watch all my favourite films at home. Anytime I want to."

He grunted.

As they stepped out into the parking lot, the bitter wind struck her face with a resounding slap. She was brought back to the present: to the clickety-clack of stilettos scratching marks on the pavement and goose-fleshed girls parading under the neon lights; to drunken boys swearing and swaggering in leather jackets; to a life thousands of miles away from home.

Lata sat in the car and burst into tears. Soon black rivers streamed down her cheeks. She shook as she wept, and Anuj sat there, fiddling with the car keys. He looked away into the distance, to the steady flicker of neon lights coming from the Bay. He waited till she dried her eyes and then started the car.

"You alright?" he asked quietly.

She patted his hand and replied, “Yeah, I’m alright. Let’s go home.”

Table Manners

The Chinese family across the street is cooking. The whole street knows. Into this cold grey evening they infuse the smell of garlic and lemongrass. The steam from their bubbling pots condenses on their window, creating a soft blur of their movements.

Their bin flew open one blustery day, spewing out oriental delights into our bleak world. Crumpled green-tea packets, golden peanut biscuit wrappings and red rice noodle cartons. Ribbons with calligraphic writing fluttered in the trees for days.

The little girl often plays on the street and when her mother calls out to her, her voice sounds like the clink of ice in a cocktail drink. This is my favourite time of day because they are all home for tea. I open the window to a slight crack and take in deep breaths. I don't know what they actually eat, but it's certainly smells better than my cling-film wrapped cottage pie.

I like to close my eyes and imagine their table. Noodles, surely, wound expertly on chopsticks, with a dark plum sauce and pork. That's what I've seen on TV. I love my Masterchefs and Bake Offs. So why is my korma never so inspiring, nor my toad-in-hole appetising? Is it because they take two minutes to heat in the microwave?

When my missus died, I just ate and ate, and grew larger and larger until I could barely fit into my armchair. What would she think, seeing this mountain who used to be her husband? I couldn't move without getting breathless and needing to sit down. The doctor says it's bad for my heart. So be it. I'm just fine sitting by the window, watching the world go by. And one day, I see a new face at the window opposite.

She's tiny, this old lady with deep wrinkles lining her face. She catches my eye and gives me a gummy smile. She has two yellow teeth sticking out from the corner of her mouth. She must be the girl's grandma, come to visit, I think. She waves and turns away.

*

She's outside my door, motioning me frantically to her house. She's pulling at my hand, talking very quickly. I lumber out, leaning on my stick and follow her. I'm still in my vest and trousers and I am aware that I smell. I haven't washed as it is such a hassle to. I enter their house unsure of what's happening. The old lady takes me out to the garden and points to a tree. A cat is sitting up there.

She's stuck, is she? I ask her. The old lady nods her head vigorously. If I can stretch my arm as high as possible and poke the cat with my stick, she'd probably jump. It takes a lot of effort to jab and shake the branch, coaxing all the while to the bloody cat to jump. We struggle for about fifteen minutes. Sweat's pouring down my face, and my arm has turned numb. I am about to give up when the cat yowls and lands on my shoulder and then scoots straight into the house.

The old woman yelps with relief, her string of words unintelligible to me but I get that she's happy. She bows to me and I feel the red burn creeping up my neck. She takes my hand and leads me in, talking all the time. I nod, as though I know exactly what she's saying.

She sits me down at the table and offers me tea, I think. It is yellow with flowers floating in it, and it smells like compost my missus used to make in the bottom of the garden. I press my lips together in a smile and wonder how to get rid of the stuff without offending her. I'm still in my vest and sweating profusely. My body hurts with all the effort I've had to put in. I really need to go home, I say. She nods, showing me her two teeth again and pours some more of the tea.

I shake my head and lean further back. I'm afraid the chair will not bear my weight. I feel my heart squeeze tight somewhere inside my chest. I shouldn't get upset, I keep reminding myself. I should go, really. But she's gaping at me, nodding and smiling. My head starts to swim. I need fresh air. The kitchen's too hot. There are pots bubbling on the stove, with enough steam to make all my fat start to melt.

She stands back, understanding my refusal. When she looks at me, I see the loneliness in her eyes. I understand what it feels to be cut off from the world you were once used to. I want to ask her so many questions—about her life, her home, her family back in China. But there are no common words to share. And even if there were, would I have actually said them? Slowly, she moves to the cooker and tends to the pots. She stirs, tastes, and adds more soya sauce. There are too many things in the room. Tins and tins of food. Blue plastic bags with some kind of leaves spilling out on the dining table. Chopped carcass of a chicken on the cutting board, a steel cleaver gleaming in the kitchen light. Calendars with Chinese numbers and photos untidily tacked on the fridge. Red fringed decorations hanging on the walls. A big paper lantern floating above me.

I watch her. Her rhythmic motion brings a sense of calmness. I like it better when she's ignoring me. She adds the vegetables to the pot. I like the pungent smell that fills the room. Slowly, I hobble towards the cooker. So what do the Chinese cook for their tea?

She welcomes my interest and speaks with a speed that if it was English, I would have a hard task to follow. She points to various bottles and pastes, making furious actions to describe their uses and effects in the cooking process. She offers me a ladle with some soup to taste. I pass so she sucks noisily from the ladle and confirms that it tastes the way she wants it to. When she finishes, she motions me back to the table. She takes the offending tea away and sets down a place for me. She serves the soup in little bowls.

"Chi, chi," she cackles, lifting up the spoon and making actions of eating. She smacks her lips and I cannot control my hunger.

We sit down and eat. My first home cooked meal in a very long time. She slurps and licks and chews noisily. I follow her lead. The cat purrs contentedly in her basket, grooming herself and yawning, like nothing had happened just some minutes ago.

After the meal, she takes a framed photo of the family and shows it to me. She pokes a bony finger at the woman, who is smiling at the camera. Her eyes are so slanted when she smiles that they look like hyphens on her face. Her smile is full of teeth. She's the mother, I recognise her. I haven't ever seen her so up close before. The old lady strokes the woman's hair in the photo, and I realise that's her daughter. The man, with his thinning hair, isn't grinning as much. He's peering through his glasses, looking like he is wasting time posing. He should be somewhere else, there is a restlessness in him. And their little girl looks more like a porcelain baby doll. She kisses the baby and places the photo on the mantelpiece again. She smiles at me. She folds her hands together and nods.

I take my leave and shamble along to my door. It's time for her to pick up her grand-daughter from school. It is time for me to doze in my chair and wait until the evening soap. But first, I wash my face and put on a shirt. Next time, I don't want to be caught unawares. There is a photo of the missus and myself on a beach somewhere that I pull out from under the bills and letters in the kitchen drawer. We are smiling, and I am half the size I am now. I wipe it clean and place it on the mantelpiece. I should look at it more often, I promise myself. I settle myself in, and smile. I realise that today I haven't heard my microwave go 'ping'.

That Face, Like a Harvest Moon

Manju sat at the head of the table, cup of strong tea in her hand, and watched her daughter and son-in-law prepare breakfast. They stood shoulder to shoulder, one cooking eggs, the other pouring coffee. She absorbed the scene, determined to take this memory back home with her. She had only a week left of her three-month stay in their home in Wimbledon.

Over the years, she had come to love Tom. She was embarrassed now at how she'd objected to Nisha marrying him. She couldn't accept a foreigner for a son-in-law. How could Nisha, from a small town in the Garo hills, cope with a man from London? She had left the hills to get a degree in medicine but came back with a husband. Their marriage wouldn't last, Manju had been sure of that. But they had proved her wrong. And together they had created a beautiful grand-daughter for her. Divya, the light of her life.

She missed having Divya around for much of her visit. She was reading English and History in Southampton. She came back for a couple of weeks over summer but then took off again. Travelling with friends. Glastonbury. Camping out there in the mud and rain. She was also volunteering, knitting hats and scarves for a cancer charity. And prosthetic breasts, for women who lost theirs to cancer. Imagine that. Divya had shown Manju one of her creations, but she had felt too embarrassed to admire the fine handiwork in front of the entire family. Especially as Divya had displayed all the woollen breasts on the dining table like frosted cupcakes offered up for tea.

"They look like pin cushions," Manju had said later, running her fingers over a pink and green striped breast, the areola a brighter pink and pointy. "Who would wear these, Divya?"

"They are very much appreciated, Nani," she had said. "They are in great demand. My tutor was diagnosed with cancer earlier this year. We all decided to do something to raise awareness and actually do something useful in our lives." She had brushed it off, but Manju had seen the look of determination in her eyes.

Manju thought guiltily about the one she had in her sewing box, which she *had* used as a pin cushion. It was one that Divya had discarded for not being perfect. She made a mental note to remove the needles from it.

The phone rang. Tom picked it up, balancing it against his chin as he dished out the eggs. He was quiet while he listened. Then he walked out into the garden. Nisha looked out of the window, raising her eyebrows in question. Divya, he mouthed and turned his back to her.

Tom returned to the kitchen and placed the coffee cup carefully on the table. Divya was not feeling too good, nothing to worry about she had reassured him. She had just cancelled her cycling trip to Wales and wanted to spend the week at home, especially since her grandmother would be leaving for India soon. Manju was pleased that Divya wanted to see her before she went. It had saddened her that her grand-daughter had more exciting things to do rather than spend time with her grandmother. Who knew when she would see her next? Immediately she began planning dishes she would cook to fatten her up. Tom said he would pick her up on the way back from work.

Manju and Nisha settled down to discuss the menu, before she too left for her afternoon shift at the hospital. Manju savoured the moment of sharing the kitchen space with the familiar smells of simmering meat and potatoes, the burning of eyes due to chopped onions and chillies. Of those peaceful days in the hills, when her husband was alive and goat meat was delivered fresh to the door. When travelling across oceans was still an improbable dream. When the local doctor was still interested in Nisha's hand in marriage. Those days, she sighed. Those days.

Manju took a stroll around the garden. It was a good year for growing, and the vegetable patch heaved with courgettes and broccoli. She twisted off young French beans and cut salad leaves, thinking of a last-minute addition to the meal. The aroma of curried lamb wafted out, and she breathed it in deeply. If she shut her eyes, and kept still, this moment could transport her back to the time when she was a girl. And her mother's beef stew pulled her like magnet from the playground to the dinner table every evening. Manju sighed. She hoped to create a sense of warmth and welcome for Divya the same way her mother had, all those years ago.

The gate clanged, and Divya walked in from the side. She looked pale and drawn. She went up to Manju and embraced her. Manju inhaled her grand-daughter's fragrance. She smelled of apples and honey. But she felt fragile, her skinny arms circling around Manju's shoulders.

"You are here, Divya! Why didn't you wait for your father to pick you up?"

"I took the earlier train. I've texted him," Divya said, putting her rucksack down.

"Good you are here. I've cooked your favourite pakoras today. You need to fatten up, child," Manju said. "All this running around doesn't do anyone any good. When did you have a proper home cooked meal? And I mean daal chawal sabzi. Not your fish and chips and burgers and pizzas. Didn't your mother teach you to cook?"

Divya smiled a little, but her eyes brimmed up.

"Thanks, Nani. That's why I came back. So you could cook for me," she said, her voice trembling. She picked up her rucksack and heaved it back onto her frail shoulders. She turned and sprinted towards the house.

"Are you ok, beta?" Manju called after her.

The afternoon passed slowly. Divya stayed in her room, Manju could hear the TV on full blast. What was the point of her coming if she didn't even want to spend time with me, she thought. She was sure there was something else going on, but she couldn't figure out what. When Divya finally came down, her eyes were red and swollen. She refused the cup of tea Manju offered her. She didn't even look at the cauliflower pakoras, her favourite, that her grandmother pushed hopefully in her direction.

"What's wrong, Divya?" Manju asked. "You don't seem ok. Tell me, I'm your Nani, na?" She reached out and stroked Divya's arm, tentatively following the raised vein up to her elbow.

Divya jerked her arm away. She opened her mouth to say something, but then rushed from her chair and ran into the toilet. Manju heard her retching, and sobbing. No, it wasn't sobbing. It was a low keening sound that made her shudder. She knew that sound very well. And she understood.

Manju retreated further away from the toilet. She did not want to know. Her heart beat so fast, she was afraid of passing out. What had that stupid girl done? Just at the threshold of her future, and now this? All those trips with her friends. All that freedom. She had known it was not right to give a young girl so much freedom. But how could she have said anything. Her parents had allowed her, and let her dig a hole into which she had fallen. Dragging the entire family with her. Her bright future was now smothered into darkness. She was ruined now.

Manju felt nauseous. The smell of the food in the kitchen made her feel sick. Her head was spinning, confusion and fear abounded. She started to clear away the table. Something to keep her mind busy. The plates clattered as she threw them into the dishwasher. She scrubbed the kadhai in which she had fried the pakoras. Scrubbed hard until her fingers bled from the steel wool scraping into her skin.

"Divya," she shouted, throwing the pan back into the sink. "How could you do this to yourself? How could you do this to your parents?"

She ran out into the garden, gasping for breath. The agapanthus swayed in the breeze, oblivious to the tension. Bright orbs of tomatoes hung from the vines. The roses spread their delicate fragrance throughout the garden. Manju was transported back home, to where orchids once grew wild. She thought back to those days of secrecy. When she, heady with the rush of first love, had broken a few rules herself. She wrung her hands in desperation. How could this happen? She would have to discuss it with Divya, see if they could make some sense out of it. Be strong, she commanded herself. Be strong.

Divya broke the news to her parents. Manju stayed up in her room, unable to face them, or the truth. She was afraid of the answers. She was afraid of Nisha's pain. Divya's pain. What of Tom? How would he react? Would he scream and shout and rain abuses on his daughter, never speak to her kindly again? Would he threaten to banish Divya from his sight? Would he force her to abort the baby? The very thought shook her to her core. She clamped her teeth tight to stop herself from screaming. She tried to concentrate on listening downstairs. She could hear quiet voices, crying, but no shouting. Perhaps they were more civilized than she could ever be. Perhaps they had sorted a way out.

*

A week later, Manju's bags are packed. She's leaving. Going back home. There have been tears, reconciliation, forgiveness. A decision has been made. Divya has decided to have the baby. Nisha and Tom have promised to support her in every way. They want to meet her boyfriend. He'll come over before the autumn semester begins. They think that it is difficult for Manju to accept such a situation.

But they don't understand, really. They don't know.

She is relieved the baby is allowed to live. She will then, set her eyes on her first great grand-child.

As Tom drives her to the airport, they sit silently in the car. She counts superstore lorries to take her mind off thinking. She hates these moments before separation. Will they meet again? She always wonders. The radio is tuned to Classic FM. The music soothes her. It is familiar music. Her father played the violin. Her father, who meant everything to her, has become a hazy image in her mind. But she can still hear him play Bach's preludes. In front of the fireplace on cold, wintry nights, he played his music with utter dedication and love. She sees his silhouette against the fire, swaying as he plays.

But the music rises to a cacophony. To the screams and anguish. To the excruciating pain. He had played and played, to drown everything out.

Stop, oh stop. Manju grits her teeth, pressing her hands to her ears. I don't want to listen to this. Tom turns off the radio. He asks if she is okay. Manju's breathing is shallow. She leans back and tries to calm down. Not now. Not now.

Tom drives into a service area and pulls up. She asks for coffee, and watches his back as he sprints across the car park. She feels a chill in the car, and pulls her cardigan closer. The sky is criss-crossed with planes, manmade shooting stars weaving patterns on the inky black canvas. And gracefully, like a dream from a faraway time, the moon rises from behind the services. Majestic and untainted, floating up to the stars. She watches, mesmerised.

Her hands instinctively touch her stomach. She has always felt emptiness there. For months she had watched it grow, too afraid to accept what was happening. Maybe it would disappear. She would wake up one morning to find herself pure and untouched. Her body unchanged. But that was not how it was. Her body changed. She had believed they would be together forever. They would have this baby, and everything would be okay. But of course, it could never end that way. He was not what her parents had in mind for her. No village boy could claim the position of their son-in-law. And certainly not one who had romanced their daughter. They had bigger plans for their only daughter.

The devil himself is inside you, her mother had cursed, watching her writhe in agony as they tried their best to finish it off.

Manju remembers that time in third person. Like it had happened to someone else. She had indeed shifted out of her body, floating somewhere in the space directly above her, watching herself. Hating herself for letting it happen. Calling out his name, again and again. Not knowing he had been beaten black and blue by her uncles and cousins. Had been forced to leave the village with threats never to return. There would be no fairy-tale ending. Only an ending, that was all.

A child without a father's name, growing inside her. A tumour, that had to be cut and got rid of. A shame never to be mentioned again. Who would have known that one day, in another land such things could be possible? That an illegitimate child could be accepted with love and dignity? She wished for that forgotten child, born so many years ago, such love. Such acceptance. But when her baby was born was born, they had taken her away. She never got to hold that baby.

But she remembers that face. It comes to her in her dreams, even today. That face, like the harvest moon, slipping out of her reach. Out of her life and disappearing into nowhere. Somewhere. She never knew where.

Her parents never spoke about that child. It was as if she had never existed, never appeared on their horizon that night, on the twenty-fifth of May, when the owls hooted among the trees, and the wolves bayed in the distant hills. It was as if that blood-stained mattress never bore the proof of her pain. It burned silently in the backyard, thin wisps of cotton catching the summer breeze. Making the air smoky and stinging the eyes. Her swollen body, leaking milk and tears, healing slowly behind the heavily barred door of the servant's room. The reality transforming into a dream. The evidence and her first love disappearing into thin air.

And once again she is at a loss. The face she has sought after all these years, the tiny face that had looked up at her for a few moments, recognising her as the mother, has appeared in Divya's womb once more.

Tom returns with two Styrofoam cups. He asks again if she's okay. He looks quite shaken by her earlier reaction. He tells her not to worry about Divya. He gives Manju his word that he will protect and look after his daughter, and help support the baby to the best of his ability. He tells her that she must find it in her heart to forgive Divya and embrace the situation. It will be better that way.

She touches his arm in gratitude and blesses him. You are a kind man for understanding your daughter's situation, she reassures him and points to the moon. Such is god's creation, she says. Unblemished. Perfect in every way. They sit in silence, watching the moon, the coffee steaming in their hands.

They reach the airport. Before getting out, Manju takes Tom's hand in hers. Thank you, she says. You are precious, my son. Look after your family, our family, well. He embraces her. Holds her to him like a child who needs confidence and strength from his mother. She gives him all she has, squeezing out every ounce of goodwill from her body. She takes off her gold chain with the diamond solitaire—her mother's—and slips it into his hand.

For Divya's child, she says. My great-grand child. My little piece of that moon.

The Summer of Learning

When Lali stole Dad's money, she also stole my childhood. I was on the trip of a lifetime. My Dad's family, tucked away in a little town in India, might as well have been on a different planet. I'd never seen them, until this summer when Dad managed to save money for 'the trip' he had been planning for ever since I could remember.

We arrived one hot sweaty night. The air was so muggy I felt I was breathing something solid. It buzzed with insects like mustard seeds swirling in a hot, thick soup. Mam was quiet, and that was unusual. She looked straight ahead, ignoring the bustle and noise around us in the railway station that smelled of diesel oil and piss. I pulled my overnight case, its spotless candyfloss pink looking proud among the dusty, battered suitcases piled carelessly on top of the porters' heads.

We spent the first night in a hotel in New Delhi, before the train journey to Dad's hometown. Mam was finally excited. She'd never stayed in a hotel before. A room with '*Ateched bathroom and running hot water*' as the advert promised. We took endless cold-water showers, just to cool ourselves. The hot water, supposedly a selling point, was wasted on us. We lounged on the crisp cotton sheets and ordered room service of big tandoori chicken legs and real naan bread, and watched Indian telly.

But the train journey was something else altogether. There was no proper toilet on the train, just a hole to aim and shoot while being jolted about in a stinky cubicle. We crossed our legs tightly together and stared out of the window to look at vast fields and villages whizz past us. The water bottle remained untouched for the next few hours. Just to be on the safe side.

Dad's brothers came to collect us from the station. This was a big event in their lives, dad had explained to us before. He always felt a sense of such pride that he was the one who had broken the ties, dared the step out of the family comforts and go explore the world. I wondered how they would take to us. I was not brown like them; I was white, with blondish hair, like Mam., though now she looked red and blotchy in this miserable heat. It made her look ugly, but she really wasn't. The men hugged my Dad, laughing loudly, slapping backs and talking in a language I understood only a smattering of.

The house was big and sprawling. It had a courtyard where chicken ran and pecked at the dust. A dog, so thin I could count its ribs, hung around, ready for some crumbs. I was told to always keep the main gate closed, or else the goats and cows would come in and eat the shrubs. I was shown the toilet at the far end of the courtyard, and my bladder shrank. I'd have to sleep in my cousin Renu's room. We were the same age, yet she was half my size. She stroked my skin and my hair like I was a Barbie doll or something. She looked like she was dipped in chocolate, her skin was so smooth and glossy. I wanted to lick her arm, to see if she tasted like chocolate too.

The ladies openly gawked at my Mam. She had decided to wear a salwar kameez to blend in. But that made her stand out even more. She towered over the tiny ladies who surrounded her and giggled behind their veils. I wished they'd give Mam a chance. They were not mean, in spite of their nudges and smiles. They welcomed her into their world. Conversation was a brisk sign language and charades, and English words rolled out so weirdly by their foreign tongues, they sounded like nothing we knew. But they gave Mam and me head massages, though I think it's only because they wanted to touch our golden hair. They painted intricate designs on the palms of Mam's hands and dressed her up as a bride. Dad hadn't brought his bride home after the registry office marriage in Cardiff. So they'd have a grand celebration here, they decided. Mam laughed when she looked at herself in the mirror. She did look so beautiful, like a princess in her chiffon and silk sari, bindi and jewellery. Not a dinner lady at a school in Riverside. Hair tied back, apron on, clearing up dishes and sick in a faded lunch hall.

Lali was the cleaning woman here. No, she was more a girl, not much older than me. She said she'd been married when she was ten. She had a little baby now, who was doped on opium to keep him asleep while she worked through five houses during the day. Her husband was an old alcoholic who sat on a charpoy all day and shouted curses at whoever passed by his hut.

Lali had dark skin and was thin as a stick. But she didn't look like chocolate. She was more like the cowpat the women smacked on the walls to dry. I felt guilty just looking at her. She sang as she scrubbed blackened pots with coconut husk and ash. Her teeth flashed white when she grinned at us, Renu and me, as we played hop-scotch in the courtyard. Sometimes she'd join in for a few minutes, laughing like any teenager, her ankle bells tinkling as she jumped, until a shout from the kitchen brought her back to her real world.

Mam rarely left her bedroom during the day, the heat and humidity had got the better of her. Her stomach couldn't cope with the spicy food and the metallic tasting water. She stopped eating at dinnertime for she didn't want to visit that toilet in the night, with spiders as big as your palm dotting mouldy walls.

Dad was out most of the time. All his brothers, cousins, friends, neighbours surrounded him, took him to parties and bars. He paid, of course. Dad paid for everything. He took his father to the doctor, had a series of tests done. It was his duty as a son to look after his parents. He paid for new saris and make up for the women in the family. He paid for gifts for the children. I understood now why it had taken so long for Dad to visit his family. It was not just the plane fare. It was everything that followed.

We had foreign money, so of course we were rich. They didn't realise we lived in a poky flat above a shop. We didn't have servants to clean up after us. We didn't eat meat and fresh vegetables picked from our land every day. Dad worked nights, driving his taxi. Mam did two jobs, caring for an old lady after her day job at the school. I warmed frozen meals and fed myself after school. I wondered if they understood who the privileged ones were.

I thought of my Nanna, smoking and swigging wine as she watched her evening soap. I loved my Nanna Carwen, her loudness, her silly jokes, her burnt dinners. Her amazing Welsh cakes. Her red heels and bleached hair. She tucked me into bed when I slept over and I loved the smell of stale smoke mixed with her strong perfume when she bent down for a cwtch. She sang me Welsh songs and when I asked her what they meant, she'd often laugh and say it was her version of the language that no one would understand.

This grandmother was so different. I had to call her Dadi. She liked to lean back on cushions on the veranda and supervise everybody. She chewed paan, offered by one daughter-in-law while the other pressed her feet. She had a sharp tongue and used it well. My aunts tip-toed around her, always waiting on her, hanging on to every word. But she too liked music and often got the dhol out and sang in a foreign language while the other women clapped and accompanied her. She gave me gold earrings. I had to touch her feet and say thank you. She stroked my hair and kissed my forehead. I got the feeling she liked me.

Things got bad between Mam and Dad. He started coming home late, and very drunk. When she protested, he yelled. He made sure everyone in the house heard him shouting at his wife. It brought him the respect he needed them to see. It brought me shame. Dad was so gentle and quiet back home. It was like a monster had been unleashed. He was performing to please his family, and getting further and further away from us. It was a mistake, he said. Coming back. Marrying Mam. Bringing us here. His rants were becoming confusing. What was the mistake? I didn't really get it.

And then Lali stole the money. Dad came raging out of his room one morning, waving his wallet in the air. Two hundred pounds. All gone. Everyone gathered around, shocked. Who would dare steal so much? Mam was livid. She swore under her breath, and I was worried they'd hear and judge her. I looked at Renu, distressed. She looked back at me, a knowing look in her eye. It wasn't long before they zeroed in on Lali. They shook her frail body, threatened her. Did you take the money? Did you steal, you useless creature? At first she denied it. And then she gave in. She fell to the floor, squirming and wailing. She held on to Dad's feet, begging for mercy. She'd taken it for her baby. He was ill; she needed money to take him to the doctor. She just took some money from his wallet, she didn't know how much it was.

I watched her grovelling at Dad's feet and felt ashamed. No one should have to do that. She was desperate for her child. Any mother would stoop to that, wouldn't she? I remembered once I had to lie to the bus conductor saying I was not yet five, when I was six, so not to pay for the ticket. Mam had made me lie. Should she have been punished too?

Lali returned what money she had left after selling fifty pounds to the local moneylender for her baby's treatment. She was kicked out of her job. Another young woman filled her place. Mam decided she was going home, whether Dad wanted to follow or not was up to him. I didn't want to go, yet. In spite of all the drama, there was something that held me back.

I didn't want to go back to my cold room and stare at the telly for ages until Mam got back from work. I wanted her to dress in colourful clothes and gossip and cook and clean like these women. I wanted hot meals cooked on long, slow fires. I wanted to aim stones at mangoes and suck the juicy flesh out of the skins. I wanted Renu to giggle with at night and play with my hair. But I too would have to return to where I came from.

On our last evening, as we waited for our bags to be loaded in the car, I spotted Lali among a group of people walking purposefully, carrying a stretcher on their shoulders. They were chanting "Ram Ram Ram" or something like that. Lali was in a white sari. She came running up to my grandmother and sobbed. Her son had died. They were going to cremate him. My breath stuck in my throat. Her baby was dead. Was that her punishment for stealing? Her eyes were red from crying, her face pinched.

She bent down and grabbed my feet. I'm sorry, she wailed. I'm sorry I stole your money, but he's gone now, my little babu is gone. Someone wrenched her away from me. I couldn't see as my eyes were blurred with tears. I heard my grandmother speak soothingly yet firmly to her. She could come back to the house after we had gone. She pressed some money into her hands. Lali nodded and then disappeared.

'After we had gone'. They were waiting for us to go. We had created a hiccup in the smooth running of their lives. Us, with our foreign money and Western ways. Things would get back to normal after we'd left. I was angry, thinking of all the sacrifices my parents had made to make this trip happen. I wasn't sure if things would be okay between Mam and Dad again. What would happen to us, after we were gone?

I watched the little group shuffle down the lane, the baby bundled on that stretcher, covered in flowers. Lali was somewhere in that crowd, crying bitterly for him. I hoped she would have another baby. I hoped that Mam would forgive Dad for bringing us here. I hoped that Dad would belong to us again. I hoped I'd never forget the taste of ripe mango on my tongue or the caress of Renu's fingers in my hair.

I lugged my pink suitcase up to the car. Sometime during our stay, it had lost its shine. It looked dusty and drab like everything else around me.

The Luxury of Quiet Contemplation

It is just a matter of wrong placement, of which foot should follow the next, that has her flat on the floor. Before she knows it, her perspective has changed and now she is looking at her kitchen from the point of view of an ant. At first, she doesn't feel anything. Perhaps she can slowly ease herself up and continue towards her destination, which is the light switch on the opposite wall. But movement evades her. Her mind orders, but limbs refuse. Her cheek is pressed firmly to the floor and she feels its cool touch on her skin.

Moments of panic. Her eyes dart from here to there. The telephone—beyond her reach. The window—too high up. Her glasses—under the kitchen cabinet. Once the panic subsides, pain sets in. Her foot hurts where she has twisted it. Her face stings where she has made contact with the floor. She squeezes her eyes shut, and tears trickle out involuntarily. Is this going to be her end? Alone in her flat, on the kitchen floor with life leaking out of her?

Her body sags as she let go. The coolness of the tiles comforts her. It is going to be a long night. If only she could have switched the light on before she fell—now she'd have to lay in the dark. As the evening deepens outside, the sounds of children playing and cars returning home subdue and die down. Smells of various dinners being cooked waft in, and she can hear the sizzle of the oil and the thunk of metal spatulas briskly stirring curries. She can smell fresh rotis being cooked on open flames. The aroma wraps around her reassuringly. Reminding her of her own prowess at turning out the perfectly rounded and puffed up rotis every single time. White light from the compound's street lamps bathes the kitchen. Her gaze remains fixed on the store cupboard, and the crumbs underneath where the maid never cleans. Brisk movement makes her realise cockroaches are scuttling out for their dinner. At least, she is not alone. For once, she welcomes their presence.

She thinks of the night he passed away. Thank goodness he had gone in a dignified way. In his bed, in his sleep. When she had woken up in the morning, she hadn't once thought of the awkward position he was lying in. She had rushed to open the door for the milkman and then to the kitchen to boil the milk. It was only after she had made tea and wondered why he was not up yet, gargling loudly into the sink that she made her back to the bedroom. But it was all finished by then. He had become a memory.

Their son and daughter-in-law had rushed back for the funeral and dutifully taken her back with them. But now the bright lights and green parks of their city held no charm for her. Those visits, made bearable with her husband for company now became a dreaded one. She wanted to be alone, cocooned in his memories, but instead she found herself having to make an effort every day to be normal. To be civil, compliant in her son's wife's house. Her son's wife. Why, she had made the choice, so she shouldn't complain. She had sifted through hundreds of photos and proposals, complacent in the knowledge that she could have any one of them, or not. They all wanted her son, a young doctor with a great future ahead of him. Green card holder. And she chose *her*. For her dark hair and fair skin. Her classically trained voice. Her degree in business management. She would be worthy of her son.

But would she be a worthy daughter-in-law? She hated living under her daughter-in-law's roof. Was this the docile girl whose voice quivered when she met them for the first time? Now she yelled at her son without any hesitation. She never waited for her him at mealtimes, like she had done for her entire married life. There were no mealtimes, eat on the go, they kept telling her. While she waited and waited, hunger gnawing at her stomach, until they returned from work.

Her son doesn't have any complaints about his wife. So maybe it is her problem after all. A problem that travels through every generation. She remembers the only woman she feared in her life: her own mother-in-law. That caustic tongue. That pointing finger. Nothing was good enough for her. She was reprimanded for being too modern, when all she had done was go to the cinema with her husband. Wear flowers in her hair, perfume on her blouse. She had cried her pillows wet, wallowing in self-pity, knowing her husband would calm her down with hungry kisses. He'd tell her to ignore his mother and to forgive her. She was just jealous. She was a widow and would never enjoy the company of a man again. Leave her alone, he would say.

Perhaps she too, in her day, had been too modern for her mother-in-law. Too forward and un-daughter-in-law like.

Yes, leave her alone, she thinks. She misunderstood her son's wife as well, she is sure of that now. There is also another side to the story. She works hard. She earns a lot of money. She makes her husband laugh. She is a good hostess to all his dinner parties. She's not how she wants her daughter-in-law to be. Submissive. Eager to please. She should accept her the way she is because she is good for her son.

A dog howls in the distance. A series of loud barking follows. The sounds of the night which she had never paid attention to before. The watchman's stick tap-tapping as he makes his rounds. A transistor somewhere with a Hindi song crackling into the air. The scurrying of the cockroaches as they criss-cross the floor. If she ever makes it through the night, she decides, she's going to give the maid the sack.

But really, how can she blame that poor woman? She had come in the other day, one side of her face purple. Husband beat her, she had said, matter-of-factly. Because she didn't have money for his drink. She had asked for a loan. She had wanted to refuse. But that would have meant more beatings. Now the maid owes her money but that hasn't changed her slip shod cleaning methods.

Her feet have gone numb. There is a consistent throbbing, but no pain. She tries to move, but her body doesn't respond. She's beginning to get quite stiff, and she's thirsty. The water filter just there, shining in the reflected light. She licks her lips and looks away. God is testing her for all her mean actions in life. Bad thoughts, bad actions, now is the time to pay up for them.

She remembers guiltily how she had not been happy when her son got his green card. It meant he would never return. Her husband had been more graceful. It was time the son went out to fend for himself. He couldn't remain tied to her apron strings forever. She had been offended. What apron strings? She had never tied him down. There were so many good jobs in this city. What was wrong with the city of his birth? But he slipped through her fingers. He belonged to another city. Another country. Then he belonged to another woman. Another life. Without her.

She hears low voices outside. She wonders what the time is. Her body is cramped and cold. She still can't move. Could she have suffered a stroke? She doesn't know the signs. Her heart beats louder in this vacuum. Can she ever get up? Her work here is done; her grandson too far away for her to love. She doesn't even understand his American drawl. He's seen her only once, he doesn't care for her presence. She should really go, she thinks. It's best for everyone. Otherwise once more, she'll be on a plane to *that* place. Fear grips her. That is the worst possible situation. Tears fall once more. She is no longer in a position to make her own decisions.

Birdsong. Pigeons hopping on the grilled window, gurgling and cooing. Sparrows chirping. What sweet sound. Golden fingers of sun creep along the kitchen ceiling. The cockroaches recede into their dark world. The clanging of milk cans on the bicycle. Sweepers brushing leaves and rubbish, the soft shush-shushing of their wide brooms on the tarmac street. Sounds of morning. Sounds of life.

The telephone rings in the living room. Her son's weekly call, early in the morning. America time. It stops. Then rings again. Silence. The milkman will be at the door any minute. The doorbell goes. The kachra-wallah to collect the rubbish. The doorbell again. Then the door banging. She shuts her eyes, willing her mind to return to that quiet place, envelope her in that dark, invisible place. There is a frenzy of activity outside. She closes her eyes, and waits.

Spider

"And this is the Andar Mahal," the guide said, pointing towards the arched doorway with a flourish. "The ladies lived here. No man was allowed to enter, except for the prince, of course."

The group followed him in. Their footsteps echoed on the cool stone floor. Pigeons roosting on the high vaults fluttered and called, their reverie broken by the sudden activity down below.

"I lived here, with my mother and sisters until I was twelve," he said. "I'm related to the prince, from my mother's side. When my father died, my mother invited by her cousin, the princess to be in her entourage."

Paula rolled her eyes and looked at her husband. He seemed to be taking it all in, like the others. She tapped her foot impatiently, wanting to get on with this boring tour and return to the hotel. A cool drink and a swim was what she was looking forward to. She didn't care about crumbling palaces and faded paintings. And certainly not this tour guide who was taking them all for a ride with his pathetic attempts at convincing them he was royalty.

"Poppycock," she whispered to her husband, who was leaning forward to catch every word the guide spoke. Paula looked at their little group. All pensioners, like herself and Tony, travelling the world before ending up in a hospice. She sniffed and turned her attention back to the guide.

Mohan Awadesh, as his badge proclaimed, sprinted forward, waving to this and that, claiming how he played with these very objects as a child. Paula sighed and dragged her feet. The others were lapping it up. They asked him questions which he answered earnestly, his black kohl-lined eyes shining. He showed them around the palace for another hour in the scorching afternoon heat. By the end, most had wilted. Paula was not only sapped of her energy but furious as well. None of this tomorrow, she decided. I'm staying by the pool. Mad elephants won't drive me out.

*

Paula kept to her word. Tony had to wander out by himself. She lounged by the pool and sipped cocktails and ate delicate hors d'oeuvres. By evening, she was in an exquisite trance when Tony walked in, Mr Awadesh in tow.

Paula struggled to sit up and struggled even further to keep her temper in check. Why was that man following Tony? Mr Awadesh grinned at her, his white teeth flashing against his chocolate skin. He bowed as he said hello. Tony was gushing with excitement. Mr Awadesh had so kindly accepted his invitation for a drink.

Of course, Paula thought. Who would pass up an invitation to a drink in a five-star hotel? "Well, I'll leave you two to it," she said. "I cannot possibly have another drink." And she wove unsteadily between the lounge chairs towards the lobby. The tour guide ran after her.

"But ma'am," he cried. "I'm here to see you. Mr Tony saying you are not enjoying my tour. I like to speak to you about many interesting things. Make you love India."

Paula spun around. How dare Tony be complaining about her to a stranger? She stared down at Mr Awadesh, who was still in a subservient stance. But his eyes had a glint. He was mocking her. She could feel it. He was inwardly laughing at her. Paula pulled herself straight and then leaned in towards him.

"I have been to India three times already," she said slowly, driving her message in. "And I must say, I have enjoyed myself thoroughly. But I will not have a tour guide tell me stories and lies just to make his tour interesting. I can see through your tricks."

"Oh, but Ma'am. I'm not lying," Mr Awadesh said.

"You are not royalty."

"Do I have to live in a palace to be a royal?" he asked. "Just because you are staying in this five-star hotel, are you a millionaire in your country?"

Paula flashed a look at Tony, who took a sudden interest in the Nataraja statue by the doorway.

Mr Awadesh put his hands together in a namaste. "I am a poor man, and I have to make a living. But I am not a liar. I am a story-teller."

Paula had to concede he was a clever man, and he had done no harm. But she wasn't going to let him win so easily.

"Okay, one drink," she said, wandering back to her seat. "What will you have, Mr Awadesh?"

"Scotch?" he suggested.

*

Paula stumbled along the stony path, trying to catch up with Mohan. Yes, after three pegs of Scotch and then some more, they had become first-name-basis friends. He had promised her he'd show her the real India. The one hidden from view. The one the travel shows avoided, the one that documentaries loved to play up. But there was more than what met the eye. He was going to show her a normal day in the life of a normal person. A day in his life.

She passed the little hutments, wary of staring eyes. People stopped their daily chores to watch them pass. She had taken great pains to dress in order to blend with the surrounding. But it was no good. Her foreignness seeped out of her camouflage. They probably smelled her out.

She passed men lathered in soap on the pavement, splashing buckets of water over their heads. She passed women squatting in front of their doorways, washing clothes and chatting with each other. There were long queues by the tube well and children jumped about in the gutters, squealing and pointing to her. Mohan marched in front, swatting children away with his black umbrella. Women giggled into their sarees and men stopped brushing their teeth to gawk. Old men, confined to their charpoys peered through soda bottle lenses to see what the excitement was about. The dogs followed, sniffing a bit too closely for comfort.

But Paula was excited. This was what she wanted. A feel for the real place. She didn't know how to react, to smile at these people or to ignore them. Mohan seemed to be enjoying it too. His thin chest was puffed out and he pushed his fake Ray Ban's up his nose while he twirled his moustache. He barked at the people who strayed into their way, choosing the choicest English swear words that Paula was sure was to impress her. She doubted these people understood what he was saying. He led her into one of the little houses. It was painted a bubble-gum pink and topped with a corrugated tin roof. A plastic door hung lop sided while a bright green curtain shielded the interior. A crowd gathered around them.

"My friend, Paula," Mohan announced to his neighbours, making a sweeping gesture towards her. Paula smiled and waved. I feel like the bloody queen, she thought. A woman stepped out of the house and glanced shyly at her.

"My Missus," Mohan said. "Lajjo."

*

It could hardly be called a house. It was one room, and a tiny kitchen. There was a big bed against the window. This doubled up as a settee. Paula sat gingerly on the edge. It felt wrong, sitting on such intimate furniture. The room was crammed with stuff. There were three tube lights, one on each wall. A small window graced the fourth wall. A television peeped out from under a pile of clothes. A transistor played Bollywood songs. Wet towels hung from hooks on the plastic door. Posters of various monuments and palaces adorned the walls, rubbing shoulders with Indian actresses pouting unnaturally at the camera. In the middle of all this clutter, a freshly ironed khaki uniform hung proud on a hanger. Official Tour Guide embroidered on one pocket. Mohan's wife stood like a statue, looking down to the floor, as if petrified to move in front of this white creature.

Paula felt large and vulgar with her red painted toenails and expensive slippers. Lajjo was thin and scrawny. Her eyes looked too big on her face. She was like a tiny schoolgirl standing in front of her head teacher. Mohan relaxed on a plastic chair, kicking his shoes off to expose dirty toenails.

"Tea?" he asked Paula. And then he laughed. "Don't worry, I bought mineral water for you. I know you foreign types scared of our water. And correctly so. Water very bad in India. You drink straight from taps in England?"

Paula nodded, embarrassed. But she was relieved he had thought of her problem beforehand. She'd have preferred a beer, but authentic Indian tea seemed promising, especially if made from safe drinking water.

"Here also, we drink from tap. See the tube well outside? Ruling party built it last year for votes. Very good locality this now. Own tube well and all. Tap water good here, but sometimes not good and then people die."

Paula didn't know what to say. She gave a bleak smile and patted the space beside her. "Come sit, Lajjo," she said. But Lajjo turned and ran into the kitchen. There was laughter and Paula noticed the neighbours peering through the window. Mohan swore at them good-naturedly and closed it shut.

"Useless people," he said. "Other people's business, their business. Bloody bastards." He used the words with pride, and watched for her reaction. Paula's eyes jerked up to meet his and she noticed the familiar twinkle in his eyes and laughed.

"Nosy parkers more like," she said. Lajjo brought out tea and samosas. She placed them in front of Paula like she was making an offering to the gods. Her gods sat on a shelf next to the steel almirah. There were dozens crammed together, laden with flowers and incense sticks and a little electric diya lamp that flickered a red electric flame.

She tucked into the samosas, their spicy filling bursting with flavour in her mouth. She'd never tasted anything like it before. She heard sizzling sounds from the kitchen and a strong smell of fish. Mohan licked his lips appreciatively. "I told her to cook you prawn pakora. Very good prawns, two hundred rupees a kilo."

*

"I take you to see someone special now," Mohan said, leading her up the street. Paula found it difficult to walk under the hot sun after the heavy lunch. Her mouth was still burning from the spicy food, but how she had enjoyed it. She wondered what Tony was up to. He had mentioned another trip into the old part of the city. More mansions and palaces. Paula was glad to have escaped that. She walked past the garbage dump, holding her breath. Goats and cows were eating scraps from there. She dodged past the cow dung dotting the road and hurried behind Mohan.

The scenery changed as they kept walking. The houses, rather shacks, spilled onto the street, making it narrow and congested. Cyclists, cows, scooters and cycle rickshaws hurtled past each other and the hundreds of people walking in the middle of the street. Here men wore skull caps and lungis, and sported orange beards. Women were covered in burkas and children had dark kohl lined eyes.

A white mosque with a green dome dominated the skyline, and in the middle of the hustle and bustle, the muezzin's call to prayer floated above in the still afternoon air. Paula clutched her scarf, preventing it from falling off her head. She hunched forward, trying not to attract attention. Dressed in her thin cotton kurta and slacks, she felt naked. Groups of women, covered in black from head to toe passed her. She felt their hands brushing against her skin. And giggles behind their veils. She never felt more exposed in her life.

*

They stopped outside a two-storey house. Mohan engaged in a hushed conversation with a man who had emerged from within. They nodded from time to time, glancing at Paula. She avoided their eye and glanced at the surroundings. This house didn't seem as rundown. It had a courtyard where hens pecked in the dirt. A woman was sweeping the concrete floor, and a few girls played hop-scotch near her.

Then Mohan told her to follow him. "He has agreed," he whispered conspiratorially. "But of course, one must give him some money."

"What are we here to look at?" Paula asked. "What does he want money for?"

Mohan blinked and climbed up the rickety stairs. It was dark. Paula followed, feeling nervous. They came to a landing, and a man motioned them to sit down. Again, there was some very fast talking in the local language. Mohan held up two fingers. "Two thousand rupees, he says."

"What?" Paula raised her voice. "I'm not paying anything. What is going on, Mohan? Where have you brought me?"

She was suddenly scared. She had trusted this man up until now but now she didn't even know where she was. And he had just done what every guide book cautioned against. *Do not part with your money. You will be cheated at every turn.* The man was staring at her, and she spotted a certain sadness in his eyes.

Mohan looked at her, defiantly. "You said you wanted to see the real India. You wanted to see what others don't. You're willing to pay thousands for a drink in that five-star hotel, and you cannot pay this man two thousand for what he has to show you? It will help his family."

By now there were other people surrounding them. Mostly women, covered in veils, but their eyes shining with interest. Paula shifted uncomfortably. Mohan had his way of making her feel rich and worthless. "Okay, I'll give," she sighed.

Once the money had changed hands, there was a shift in the mood. The women began chattering and the man smiled. They rushed inside a room and Paula could hear laughter. She heard children chattering and giggling. The curtain parted and Paula recoiled in horror. And then she felt terrible that they had seen her reaction on seeing them.

The two boys simply grinned and walked towards her with practised ease. They were joined in the head and chest, arms and legs moving in perfect co-ordination, like a spider. When one looked her in the eye, the other had to face downwards. And then they switched, and the other looked at her and grinned.

Irfan and Imran, the father announced proudly. Irfan gave her a salute and then flipped over. Imran winked at her. Paula stared at them, unable to move. How should she react, she didn't know. She was aware of the rest of the family staring at her, waiting for a reaction. A wave of anger flooded over her. How dare Mohan bring her here. These two boys were not exhibits to make money out of.

"What is this?" she hissed at him. "Why have you brought me here?"

"Because you didn't want to see monuments. You wanted to see ordinary things," Mohan whispered back.

"They are not ordinary things. This is *not* what I meant," she said.

The twins fell on the floor in a heap, arms and legs all over the place. They laughed and looked at her. Paula averted her eyes. She was not going to be entertained by this circus act. How could the parents do this to their children?

"It's ordinary for them," Mohan countered. "They not know anything else."

"Okay, but it's not right for the family to put them on exhibition." Paula said.

A young boy standing in the corner spoke up. "They are Xiphopagus twins." The words tripped off his tongue easily. "Big TV company come from America. They film my brothers. They famous in America. One lady want to take them there. Operation. Separate them."

"So why not try and do that then?" Paula said. "Separate them, give them independence."

Irfan and Imran sat down against the wall, listening intently. Irfan twisted his head to take a look at his twin, and they smiled at each other.

"But they don't mind," their brother said. "Look at it this way. They go to school. They have friends. We have five sisters who need to marry. Irfan and Imran can never get job. This is their job. Get money for sisters' weddings. They happy to do this. They happy to feed the family."

"Are you sure?" Paula raised her voice. "Have you asked them if they are happy?"

The twins crawled away, unsure of her. Paula knew she wasn't giving them the required reaction. One of disgust, awe, sympathy. But never of outrage—in their favour.

The father bent down and folded his hands together. "Happy. Happy." He said. He stared at her purse, willing it to open. He then spread his fingers out. "Five girls," he said. "Not happy."

Paula looked at the girls surrounding the father. They had pretty, young faces and were beaming at her. How could they accept their father insulting them in front of her? But then, she thought, this was reality. This was normal. And she had asked to see it. She wanted to turn and run. Run far away from here. To where the palaces were. Where the romance was. To stories of princes and princesses in all their finery dancing in the moonlight. Yes, Mohan had been right after all. Monuments and fairy-tales were far better than real life. They didn't leave a bitter taste in the mouth.

The girls giggled as their conjoined twin brothers waddled up and down the landing. They looked adoringly at the two boys. Their saviours. Paula rummaged through her purse and pulled out some boiled sweets. She thrust them into Mohan's hands.

"For Irfan and Imran," she said. "For once. Let them enjoy their earnings."

Mohan gave the boys the sweets. They whooped for joy and raced down the corridor, laughing. Their sisters followed, laughing and calling to them. The father joined his palms together and looked up to the sky. He shrugged and said thank you to Paula. She turned away and looked at Awadesh.

"Enough of this drama," she said, pressing the money into the mother's hands. "I've had enough. Now please, take me back to the hotel."

A Holiday to Remember

Rima looked around, feeling disappointed. So this was a caravan. It was quite flimsy and very cold. Certainly not worth the money, she thought.

"Look. Everything is fitted into this tiny space," Anand beamed. "Cooker, sink, microwave, fridge. Ingenious."

He pulled open the drawers and waved a fork and spoon at her.

"It's got everything you need. Just sit back and relax."

He sank into the couch and switched on the television. Anne Robinson's jibes filled the room.

Rima placed Baby on her hips and went to inspect the bedroom. It reminded her of the matchbox which she had converted into a bed for her pet snail when she was a child. It had a bed and wardrobe. No cot. Hadn't they asked for a cot?

"Anand," she called out. "There's no cot here." Baby wriggled and tried to slide down her hips.

"I know," Anand said. "I didn't ask. It's fifty quid extra. No worries, I'll sleep out here. Look, there's a sofa bed here—a mechanical marvel."

Outside the evening was quite raw. It was grey and the wind had a bite in it. The bare trees heaved and strained above the caravans.

"It's quite cold," Rima said, covering Baby with her shawl. "Turn on the heater, na."

Anand jumped up and fiddled with the gas fireplace. It came to life with an orange glow and the warmth embraced them immediately.

"Aah-ha, that's wonderful," cried Rima and tickled Baby's chin. She squealed back in delight. Anand tickled her some more, and soon they were all laughing together.

They had met in a suburban college in Bombay; fallen in love in the canteen over oil-sodden samosas and sweet milky tea. They had not thought of the consequences, just being in love was enough. But now, both were trying to come to terms with the reality.

They should never have met. Anand, in his machine-washed, designer-labelled T-shirts was a misfit in a college where most students had their clothes bashed on the bathroom floor by their mothers and hung to dry in the sun. He had not got the required percentage to make it to the college of his choice. Besides, he had been holidaying in Australia during the admission week. It really didn't matter where he got his degree from. His father's successful business would see him through life in any case.

Rima was told to go to a college within walking distance of her home. So she set off to the end of the road, umbrella held over her head to prevent her skin from darkening. The marriage market narrowed down as the darkness quotient increased.

And they fell in love. To everyone's surprise, they also got married. Anand did not abandon her to marry someone of his parents' choice.

When Rima went to live in Anand's home, she felt embarrassed: about herself, her family. Anand's family lived in a plush two-storey duplex apartment on Worli Sea Face. The walls facing the sea were made of glass. There was art on the walls that was more expensive than her parents' tiny flat in the suburbs. Anand was shocked to have to share a toilet with five people whenever he visited her family. Eventually he stopped going.

It was hard on Rima. All this lavishness made her feel guilty. That she didn't belong here. All this was meant for someone else. Someone whose father was a neurologist or a diplomat. Someone who was comfortable with Italian furniture that had to be covered in bed sheets most of the time to protect it from the Mumbai dust and damp. She no longer licked her fingers clean after a meal. Her fork and knife clattered clumsily on her fine china plate.

It dawned on them both that maybe it wasn't so right, after all. But they were young, and they were in love. And also, perhaps more importantly, Anand's mother loved Rima like her own daughter. That was half the battle won.

Then Anand landed himself a job in the UK. His parents were not so keen on their only son leaving. They begged him to reconsider. After all, whatever they had was his. They cajoled Rima to convince him. But actually, both of them thought it an excellent opportunity to escape from their differences. Make a life for themselves where they could be on equal terms. It made so much sense. And so here they were, on their first vacation, and Anand wanted everything to go right.

He was very happy to get this holiday deal so cheap. A hundred pounds for four nights. Off-season rates, no doubt, but who needed the sun? An outing to any place away from home was enough. A caravan holiday. How romantic was that!

"Let's have some tea," he suggested. Baby tumbled out of his arms and crawled towards the TV. Rima switched on the kettle and rummaged for the tea in the food basket. They had two types of tea. Anand drank Darjeeling tea, and only Oxfam Fairtrade Darjeeling tea, which was nearest to the tea he drank in India. Rima preferred the strong taste of PG Tips, with lots of milk and sugar.

She dug deep into the basket, but couldn't find the Darjeeling tea. Her PG Tips was there, but where was Anand's tea?

Oh no, Rima bit her tongue when she realised what she had done. Just before they had left, Anand had wanted a cup of tea for the road. She'd made it, and then left the box on the kitchen counter. She turned around to look at Anand, who was playing with Baby. She didn't want to spoil this holiday.

"Anand," she said. "I've left your teabags at home."

He stared at her incredulously. Like she had forgotten to bring Baby's formula, perhaps. Or like she had lost her passport. Rima was close to tears.

"It's okay," he said slowly. "I'll have coffee, no problem."

"I didn't bring any."

"Oh."

Rima wrung her hands in despair. Baby looked at her and stuck out her lower lip.

Anand swept Baby into his arms and smiled.

"I'll have whatever you have then. Good old English tea in an English caravan. Yes, Baby?"

"Ba-by," Baby lisped and squealed with laughter.

So they sat huddled by the fireplace, strong tea steaming in the cups and they watched Anne Robinson insult one contestant after another until there was none left.

The next morning, they woke up stiff and thirsty. All three had squeezed into the pull-out in the lounge. The bedroom had been freezing and by midnight Rima had crawled under the duvet beside Anand, with Baby between them. Rima was awake most of the night, afraid of Baby suffocating under the duvet. Anand, being closest to the fireplace was hot and parched all night. Yet, he smiled and reminded Rima that this was a caravan holiday, not a five-star resort, so this was how it would be and that they should enjoy it.

Rima nodded and busied herself with making breakfast. She looked into the caravan in front of theirs. There was a white family in there. The children were having breakfast. The mother was carefully applying mascara. Rima looked at her watch. 8.07 am. The woman needed to wear make-up so early in the morning? She reminded her of her mother-in-law. Never a hair out of place. Nails always manicured and covered in transparent varnish. Her mother's nails were perpetually yellowed by turmeric. She studied her own: chewed down to the skin. Ugly. She would have to buy nail-polish when she returned and also invest in a manicure.

She whisked two eggs and poured them into the hot frying pan. She made up Baby's fruit puree and infant rice mix.

"So, what shall we do today?" Anand rubbed his hands together and then attacked his omelette. Rima looked out, it was still blustery.

"It's very cold outside," she said. The family next door trudged out in t-shirts and track pants. Pink on the girls. Blue on the boy. They were giggling and talking excitedly. The mother had red lipstick. The father had a big paunch and a can of beer in his hand. Rima looked at the watch again. 9.10 am. She rolled her eyes. Baby spat her breakfast on Rima's dressing gown.

"Let's go to the Entertainment Area. There's a heated indoor pool." Anand picked up the dishes and put them in the sink. "I'll do the dishes. You get Baby ready."

The indoor pool was crowded. Children ran around, screaming and jumping into the water. Every inch of space in the pool was occupied. Baby wailed loudly and hid her face inside her mother's coat. It was too cold to take her to the playground so they wandered around the pool tables and slot machines.

Soon, it was time for Baby's nap, and they returned to the caravan. Anand watched TV with the volume down and

Rima padded about, preparing lunch. The TV had been left on in the other caravan, so she watched the Eastenders' Omnibus through the window, while stirring the instant noodles.

They spent the night cramped up on the pull-out bed once more. But feeling uncomfortable in this claustrophobic caravan made Rima feel very guilty. Her parents' flat was just as cramped, and they didn't even have the facilities so neatly fitted into every crevice of this caravan. She had been comfortable in her parents' flat, but now she knew things would not be the same again.

The next morning, they decided to go for walk along the promenade. They trundled along the path, following the signs to the sea. Baby bumped along happily in her pushchair. Rima struggled to keep her hair out of her eyes. Anand faced the wind bravely, pushing Baby against the rebellious wind. When they reached the promenade, they were disappointed. In front of them was a great, muddy flat land, the water murky in patches here and there. It was low tide and the sea had gone right out.

Anand sighed. "Nothing compared to the Arabian Sea."

Rima nodded. The sea outside Anand's house in Mumbai was different. Sometimes wild and hitting the promenade with such force that the glass windows would be sprayed with the salty water. Sometimes gentle and lapping softly against the rocks. Families, lovers, hawkers, policemen would cover every inch of the promenade. Balloons straining on their strings. Corn cobs roasting on white hot coal. Roasted peanuts in paper cones. People running, walking, laughing, holding hands, a stolen kiss perhaps, a knowing whistle.

None of it was here though. This promenade was very clean and almost empty at this hour. Bins with liners were set up neatly at equal distances. Benches with a few old men sipping their beers. A dog-walker who paused to smile at Baby. A bitter wind that threatened to blow all of this away.

Rima fiddled with Baby's blanket. Anand looked at her, his eyes questioning, what now?

She didn't reply. She hadn't worn long-johns under her jeans and she was regretting that.

"Let's have some tea in there," said Anand, pointing to a tea-room. "Maybe they'll have Darjeeling tea." Rima's eyes stung and she bent down to adjust Baby's straps.

They walked back to the caravan in silence. The tea-room had Twinings' Darjeeling, and that was *not* the real thing. So, they had coffee instead. When they reached their car, Rima wanted mineral water from the boot for Baby's formula. She moved Baby's pushchair out of the way in order to open the boot.

Suddenly a man came rushing out of the caravan near them.

"Watch out," he shouted.

They froze. Immediately they thought Baby was in danger and Rima moved the pushchair close to Anand.

"Hey, stop. You're scratching my car."

Rima looked at the man. What was he talking about? He was towering over them now, stubbing his finger on some scratch marks below the fender.

"Look what you've done," he said, his cold eyes boring into her. His thin lips were snarling, baring yellow teeth and foul breath. She leaned back.

"What have I done?" she said. Anand stepped in front of her.

"What's the problem?" he asked.

"I seen it from my window," the man yelled, saliva spraying into the fraught air. "She pushed the buggy too close to my car, and scratched it."

Anand stared at him. "What? The buggy scratched your car?"

The man nodded, examining the scarred car with his fingers.

A woman came out of his caravan, pushing a wheelchair. A child was in it. His head was twisted in an abnormal angle and his tongue lolled out. He wore thick glasses, but the eyes were unfocussed. Rima flinched on seeing him.

The woman's lips were a red slash on her thin face.

"We seen you damaging our car," she said.

"Yeah, you need to pay us compensation," the man said. The boy grunted and twitched his head. He looked about ten.

"Two hundred quid. That's the deposit on this rented car," the woman shouted, her hand absently patting the boy. "They won't give it back once they seen the scratches."

Anand bent down to examine the car. Yes, there were a couple of scratches, but surely the plastic handles of the pushchair couldn't do that.

"Listen, sir," he said. "I can see the scratches. But I can assure you it's not our pushchair that did it."

He aligned the pushchair against the car and pointed it out.

"See, it doesn't even reach where the marks are. You've made a mistake. Those scratches were already there."

The man's face turned red and splotchy. He shook his head violently. "We seen you do it. We're going to sue you. I've got your licence number."

The woman swore under her breath and wheeled the boy up the ramp into the caravan. The man jotted their licence number and marched away.

Anand placed his hand on Rima's elbow. She was shaking. He guided her and Baby back to their caravan.

"What sorts of people come here on holiday?" she asked, her voice unsteady. "Bullies."

He patted her gently and opened the door. Rima burst into tears as soon as they were inside. "Did you see their boy?"

"It's none of our business," said Anand, and switched on the television.

"But Anand, he could have been ours. Then we'd have been so angry and frustrated." She held Baby tightly to herself.

"Don't be so melodramatic." Anand snapped. "Forget about them. Bloody trouble-makers."

"But they'll sue us. What are we going to do?"

Anand laughed. "Sue us? Saying what? A bloody pushchair scratched their car? Give me a break. That bastard wanted to pass the blame on to us. Try and get the money off us. But it isn't going to work."

Rima continued to sob and Baby struggled in her grip. She held out her plump arms to her father.

"Ba-ba," she said.

Anand gathered her into his arms and sprawled on the sofa. "Make some dinner, Rima. Let's make it an early night."

"I want to go home," cried Rima. "I hate this caravan. I hate this holiday."

Anand stared at her, his ears went red. "You are so selfish," he snapped at her.

"I tried my best to have a nice break. I didn't complain that you forgot to bring my tea. I do the dishes every night. I've saved up for this holiday, and you don't appreciate it."

"Appreciate what?" Rima retorted. "Two sleepless nights on this pull-out bed? Wandering around aimlessly in this freezing weather? Is this a holiday?"

Anand stood up, his face glowering. No words came from his lips but Rima knew everything he wanted to say. Where did she think she came from? Since when did she start complaining about indecent accommodation?

He stormed out of the caravan, leaving Rima to sob loudly and Baby staring at her mother in distress.

After a while, Rima recovered. She fed Baby and played quietly with her. She regretted being so mean to Anand. He had meant only goodness. It was she who had a complex. She, who always saw the negative side to things. She played absently with Baby's toys and watched her giggle and crawl on the carpet.

Baby got on to her feet and held on to the coffee table. She looked at Rima and smiled. Two tiny teeth cradled delicately in her pink gums. She giggled and took a tentative step towards her mother.

Rima held her breath and watched.

"Come here, Sweety," she cried and beckoned baby to her. Baby curled up her toes and tottered a step forward. Then another step. Slowly she went down on the floor and clapped her hands.

Rima clapped and laughed out loud. "Well done, Baby. Well done. Once more, come on."

Encouraged by her mother, Baby tried again. One step. Then another, till she was in her mother's arms. Rima picked her up and danced around the room. She looked out of the window into the deepening twilight. She saw Anand sulking outside. She opened the door and called out to him.

"Anand, come here quick," she yelled, and waved.

He looked up, concerned and saw her beaming at him. He ran towards them.

"Baby's first steps," she laughed. "Baby just took two steps, then five. Where's the camera?"

Anand dashed to get the camera from his back pack.

"Oh Baby, show daddy what you did. Come on, come on." Rima placed Baby on the carpet and they knelt down in front of her. Then, with a look of great concentration, Baby teetered towards her father. He clapped and laughed and took a picture of his daughter. Rima leaned on him from behind to look at the LCD screen. Baby was there, one foot in front of the other, tooth shining in the flashlight, walking towards them.

"Take another one," Rima gushed. "Take another one."

"You go in front," Anand instructed her. "I'll take one with both of you."

Rima posed with Baby, giggling and victorious, just her daughter.

"Now you," she cried, and grabbed the camera. "You pose with her,"

"Anand kneeled on the floor, bending to be in the frame." Baby walked confidently towards her mother.

When Rima clicked, she captured two pearly white teeth, out of focus, but evidence enough that baby had walked right into the camera.

After She Was Gone

The phone rang.

Papa was in his usual place in front of the telly, watching Blockbusters. He had turned the volume up so high I could hear Bob Holness asking his questions. Usually I watched it with him—he said it was a good educational programme. For whom, I often wondered. Papa hadn't been to school much. Driving a taxi didn't require a degree. But tonight he had stationed me in my room, to keep a watch out of my window. I could look as far down the street to the main road. Mummy was out, as usual, but this time, she was very, very late.

I tried my best to ignore the baby cot that had been dismantled and shoved under my bed. But I couldn't. It lay there, innocently pink but I knew how evil it really was. Like a stuck record, the same thought wheeled around in my head. Why had they wanted another baby? Weren't they happy with just me? Look what baby Dolly did to us. She cried and cried, and took up everyone's attention. And then one night she stopped breathing. Just like that. In that very cot. And that's when Mummy became someone else.

Papa took the call. He didn't say a word, only nodded. Then he yelled up to me to put on my coat. I looked at him as I came down the stairs, and he seemed old and tired. His eyes were streaked with red lines, like he was crying, but his temple throbbed, like he was real angry. I remembered his temper when he caught me with a ciggy at the end of the garden and sliced my thighs with his belt. He hadn't waited for my explanation. That I had found it smouldering on the path, and had picked it up to watch it glow in my hand. But he of course didn't believe that. I was growing up to be just like them, he had yelled. Those thugs who dawdled outside the corner shop, smoking, swigging beer. A good beating would remind me of my Indian heritage, he was convinced of that.

I hurried along, wondering where Mummy was. She was definitely in trouble, for Papa was marching up the road, swearing under his breath. What would Papa do to her? I eyed his middle, that damned belt was snug below his fat belly. But I didn't dare ask him anything. As we walked towards the city centre, he told me that the security-men had got Mummy.

What security-men? Mummy hadn't killed Dolly. But was she trying to kill someone else's baby? Like Kusum Aunty's little girl. Revenge. I could believe that, since Mummy hadn't stopped cursing Kusum Aunty, saying she had cast the evil eye on her Dolly. How Kusum Aunty was always commenting on how beautiful Dolly was. How lucky we were to have another baby. She only had the one. Pinky. Who was dark and had stringy hair. Nothing pink about her. What rotten luck. Who would marry her? But Dolly was all milk and cream. Sometimes I would just sit and watch Dolly while she slept. White skin, black hair and the softest, pinkest lips. Sometimes I wished I'd have been born like her. But my face was covered with pimples and my thick glasses made my eyes look like a frog's. Mummy would curse as she struggled to tame my hair into a braid. No one would marry a girl with such wild hair, she'd say as she combed out the knots. But I lived, while Dolly died.

We didn't go to any police station. Papa strode into a department store. Already the shutters were half down. A security man looked unhappily at us. He couldn't go home until the shop was locked for the night. He was young, with ginger hair sprouting from his chin. I felt sorry for him. Surely my heavy-weight mum could have wrestled him to the floor and run. He walked up to us, back straight, almost marching.

"Mrs Singh was caught shoplifting," he said officiously. "This is her first offence?"

I could have spat on him. Papa was no longer straight and proud. He hung his head, like he was the criminal. He apologised and said yes. I saw Mummy in the corner of the security office, staring at her image on the CCTV camera. She was whimpering like a lost kitten. Her handbag was on the floor, unzipped and her stolen goods vomiting out of the bag. She wouldn't look at us, kept wiping her eyes and nose. Baby formula? Why was she stealing that?

"I thought we would need it," she said to Papa. "My milk has dried."

The security man said something about a first warning. He must have felt sorry for her. Or maybe he really had to go home and didn't want to be delayed any further. We walked out into the chilly night, not saying a word. Mummy sniffled as she followed us. Papa strode ahead, not waiting for us to catch up. I stared at my trainers and realised that I had two different coloured socks on. I pulled my salwar lower and shuffled behind Papa. Two punks jeered and called us names. I hunched inside my coat and hurried along.

That night I strained against the wall to listen to my parents. But I heard nothing. As the moon sailed across my window, I slipped out towards the toilet. On the landing I paused. I heard Mummy's gentle snores. I heard my Papa, crying softly. I wanted to go in and hold them close. Remind them that they still had me. I would never hurt them like Dolly did. If only they'd look at me and see that I was there for them.

But it didn't stop with the first warning. Mummy continued to pilfer from shops. Hairclips. Shampoo. Baby cream. Paracetamol. Gaviscon. More formula. Gripe water. She managed to avoid the security men most of the time. But sometimes, Papa had to answer a telephone call and step out to retrieve her. I wasn't made to accompany him anymore.

The doctors became involved. They said she was depressed and this was her way of asking for help. Mummy went to a counsellor. But it had to be all hush hush. The neighbours should not know. All the aunties at the gurdwara should not be able to sniff it out. They were whispering already and beginning to keep their distance. We had to pack

Dolly's clothes and toys and give them away to charity. The baby cot was pulled out from under the bed and given a good dusting. That too had to go.

Mummy took to cleaning. She scrubbed and polished and brushed and dusted. She didn't leave the house. She cooked and pickled and knitted and sewed. She stopped seeing friends and then the friends stopped dropping by. Papa sold his taxi and resigned himself to his armchair. I left them in that bubble and went to university. I studied chemistry. I became a pharmacist. I married. And then I had a baby.

It was like my parents were resurrected from the dead. They had a gleam in their eye when they held my son, Ambarjeet. Mummy made sure he had thick kohl lines drawn under his eyes. Black tikka on his cheek. To avoid all evil eyes. Because he was so fair and milky and sticky and sweet. I'd hold him to my chest, obsessing over him, inhaling his scent, cherishing his need for me. He was mine, and I spent many a night, checking his breath on my cheek, his heartbeat under my palm.

Mummy would bring him little gifts she'd made. Jumpers. Mittens. Baby shirts and bed linen. She indulged him, and Papa's laughter shook the house. At last they were happy. The happiness that had been snatched from my childhood was returned to us through my son. But that didn't last long. Mummy died. Her heart stopped in her sleep. Once again, Papa was stunned into silence.

Papa refused to move in with us. Everyone tried to convince him to do so, but he didn't listen. He just sat in his armchair and stared out of the window. He didn't eat unless I visited and warmed up some food for him. His eyes did not light up seeing Ambu toddle up to him. He shrivelled up. I watched him deteriorate and cursed Dolly. Are you happy now? Just two months of your presence and a lifetime of sorrow for the three of us. At least she had mummy now, for eternity. I wondered if finally, Mummy would be at peace, in the company of her favoured one. And then I'd berate myself for thinking that. I was a mother too. I could understand the path my mother had taken. But still, those thoughts remained.

One evening, I called as usual, but he didn't answer the phone. I panicked, imagining all possibilities as I strapped Ambu into his car seat and rushed over to him. I found the house in darkness. The gloom inside was like a thick blanket, enveloping me in its constrictive embrace. I struggled to breathe as I switched on the lights one by one, racing around the house, calling out for Papa. I put Ambu down by the stairs and shushed him as he started to protest. I heard shuffling upstairs so I ran up, afraid of what I would see.

He was sitting on their bed, bags and clothes strewn all over the floor. I turned the light on and he smiled, saying he hadn't realised it had gone dark. I'm clearing your mother's things, he told me. It's time.

I nodded. I looked at her clothes and handbags and shoes. I'd been meaning to do it ages ago, but hadn't found the strength to. I'd have to help him to stuff them into bags and take them to the charity shop now. I sighed and didn't know where to begin. But Papa held up his hand. I'll do it, he said. You have a baby to look after. I need to do this.

He pulled out a quilt from the bag. I remembered it well. A colourful patchwork quilt Mummy had made it out of scraps of my old dresses and her sarees. There were even bits of Papa's corduroy trousers in there. I smiled as I felt it between my fingers. Different textures. All different stories, patched up to make this quilt. Papa held it out to me. For Ambarjeet, he said. Your mother would have wanted it that way. He smiled kindly at me and ushered me back to my baby. I held the quilt close to me, not remembering it to feel as lumpy as it did now. I couldn't use it for my baby, but I didn't want to tell Papa that.

I cooked him dinner while he held his grandson. I portioned off the food and put them in the freezer, repeating over and over again that he'd have to eat all of it in the next few days. That I would be checking that he'd been eating. He smiled again and nodded.

Ambu started to fret. It was past his bedtime and I needed to rush back home. Papa helped bring out all my things. I managed to put Ambu in his car seat while Papa loaded the boot. It was beginning to rain and I didn't want to linger. I grabbed the buggy and dumped it on top of the quilt. We looked in horror as a mud stain spread across the cloth. I yanked the buggy off, and then heard the rip. The little patches of cloth, so old, tore easily where it had caught the wheel. We stood motionless and watched. Out fell little mittens and socks and bits of baby-gros. The quilt had been stuffed with baby clothes. Most with their tags still on. The ones that got away. The ones she stuffed quietly into this quilt. Bit by bit, padding the quilt. It must have taken her years, and yet she never got caught.

For a moment, there was complete silence. We stayed frozen, and then Ambu's cry ripped the air. Papa jolted out of his trance and picked up the fallen items from the ground. He hugged them close to his chest and stumbled towards the door.

"I'll take these," he said quietly. "I'll take them down to the charity shop tomorrow."

I watched his retreating back. He was hunched over the bits he was carrying. The rain came down harder and I jumped into the car and drove off. I didn't toot the horn like usual. This visit was best left unacknowledged.

Marked

1993

"Let's put our names here," she said, breathless in her excitement. "It will remain forever, like we will. Be together forever." She took out her nail file and waved it in front of his face.

He grabbed her hand, playfully trying to pry the nail file out of her grip. "We can't do that. It's called vandalism. Soon the whole wall will be covered in initials and love declarations. This is the Taj Mahal, not a blackboard."

"You're so boring," she laughed but surrendered to him. "I love you. You love me. I'm sure Shah Jahan would have approved."

He pulled her closer to him. She nestled in his arms, caressing him, feeling his light kisses on her neck. They stayed hidden from view, away from the crowd strolling on the grounds.

The evening swept in from across the river. Parrots hurried over the turrets, flashing emerald glints in the setting sun. The haunting sound of the muezzin's call to prayer floated through the air. The Taj Mahal glowed gold. It was closing time, and people walked towards the exit gates. Their feet dragged as if their souls did not want to part from this marble promise of undying love.

"He loved her so much he built this tomb for her," she persisted. "If we write our names here, our love will last too."

"Really, you are too naive. Do you really believe in that?" he said. "Love won't last because we scratched our names on this wall. It will last if your parents agree to us being together."

She nodded in agreement. But something told her it would not last, anyway. It made her even more adamant. She turned away from him, and scratched their initials in the marble plinth on which the Taj stood. He tried to grab her hand but she elbowed him away. She laughed nervously, avoiding his gaze.

"It's done," she said. "It's etched in time forever. No one can change that."

If one looked long and hard, they'd find the spidery writing. A hopeful promise that their love would survive the test of time. A.B. heart I.K.

2016

Anuradha squeezed her body out of the Tata Sumo, her eyes squinting in the harsh sun. The girls sprang out after her. They had remained like coiled spring in the car, but now were unleashed into the open. They too were momentarily blinded by the glare. The long journey had made them tired and irritable. Anuradha reached for her bottle of mineral water, worrying for a second that it was probably contaminated anyway. She took a small sip and grimaced.

Warm bottled water tasted vile. She watched her husband reach into his big camera bag and fumble with the various lenses.

"Wait till we get inside, na," she said. "We don't want to advertise ourselves here."

But it was too late. Bands of urchin boys surrounded them, begging for money. Hawkers elbowed in, their neck muscles taut with the load they carried on their hanging baskets.

Buy. Here. Look. Taj Mahal duplicate. Real marble. Good price sir. Only for you. Peacock feathers. For your girls. Buy. Buy. I take American dollar, sir. No problem.

Their voices warbled and droned in the heat waves and Anuradha swatted at them like they were flies.

"Look what you've done, Raj," she hissed in his ear.

He rolled his eyes and shrugged. He turned to the hawkers and beggars and held his hands up. "Sorry, boss says no."

They marched towards the gates, ignoring more pleas to buy. A monkey sauntered in front of them and the girls squealed. It held its palms up.

"I cannot ignore this one," Her husband laughed and dug into his pockets. He came up with a packet of peanuts which he scattered on the ground. The monkey rushed in and grabbed all it could. Stuffing its mouth full, it clambered up a dusty tree.

They passed through the dark gateway and suddenly there it was, falling into view. Dazzling in the sun. The effect was always startling no matter how many times she saw it. It took her breath away. She looked at her daughters, curious about their reaction. They stood close together, looking at the Taj through their phone screens. She sighed as they clicked constantly, uploading photos to their Instagram feeds.

She held her husband's hand and leaned into him. It had taken them so many years to make this plan happen. Their annual trips to India left them little time out of the usual family get-togethers to go away to sightsee. He squeezed her hand and kissed the top of her head. They let the girls wander off, taking photos of everything around them. She looked at her daughters as they walked away. Wearing shorts and t-shirts, baseball caps perched on their head and earphones plugged into their ears, they looked every inch the American tourists.

"So what do you think?" she asked him, nodding towards the Taj. But somewhere, deep down—deep, deep down, she hoped it would not make a great impact on him. She flinched at her own selfishness, her inability to share the Taj with anyone else. She had always stalled the plans to visit, perhaps subconsciously. Perhaps not.

"I have no words," he replied. "I'm speechless, literally. I can just sit here all day and stare at it. Can't you?"

He put his heavy camera bag down and sat on the grass. The crowds milled by, families out on a day trip, laughing, chatting, munching on snacks. But the Taj remained aloof, climbing up to the heavens, unmindful of the river of life streaming around it.

"Hmmm," Anuradha left him sitting there and walked on. "I'll be back in a minute."

The last time was when she had come with him—all those years ago. When she believed that they could convince their parents to accept their relationship.

He had proposed and gone to meet her parents. But that was a bad year to want to marry a Muslim. Her parents had been vehement in their disapproval. They hid behind the lame excuses of the terrorist attacks and safety for the family and being shamed in their community. He had not fought for her. And this always crept up on her—this feeling of failure. Even when she was playing with her daughters, or cooking her husband's favourite dish—a sudden flash of feeling rejected would pulse through her body. She had not been fought over. She had been let go quite easily. And nothing could ever make up for that.

She climbed up the platform and entered the arched door. It was cool inside. Her eyes followed the calligraphy and flower engravings, greeting them like an old friend. Once, these flowers had been encrusted with jewels and precious stones. The British had helped themselves to those and left behind cheap stones and painted paisleys. Why did she always think of the same annoying fact every time she visited? It pained her to think that the Taj had been looted and vandalised. It was meant to be a symbol of love.

But there was something else that she wanted to see. It had played on her mind the entire journey up the new highway from Delhi to Agra. She had replayed that scene over and over again in her head. Them, sheltered away from the crowds. Her, etching their initials on the wall. The hot marble burned her bare feet and she hopped across to the spot. Would it still be there? Like a blind person reading braille, trying to uncover the story from her past, she carefully ran her fingers along the plinth. But she couldn't find it. The marble was cool and smooth to touch. It hadn't lasted through time.

A hand touched her shoulder and she straightened. This was the man of her present, her future. This was the man she loved. She took his hand to her lips and kissed it.

But he kept staring at his phone. "UK has voted to leave," he said. "Man, this is unreal. It happened, jeez, it happened."

"Good lord," Anuradha whipped out her phone and scrolled down the screen. "They did it. Unbelievable."

She looked around, hoping to find some sort of reaction around her. But the people were oblivious to news from other parts of the world. Here, they remained ensconced in a bubble. A picture-perfect version of playing happy families. Here, the world was a happy place of taking selfies, eating picnic lunches and wandering through the scented gardens that surrounded the Taj Mahal.

Anuradha pushed the phone back into her handbag and entwined her hand in his.

"Not now, Raj," she whispered. "It doesn't concern us. For now, just enjoy this moment. This is our moment. Ours alone."

She felt a surge of emotions press against her eyeballs and was glad that she could hide behind her sunglasses. He squeezed her shoulders and then stretched his arm out to take a selfie of them. "Smile, my begum," he said. "A photo with you here is mandatory, you know. Let the world see and know."

She smiled for the camera, knowing already that this photo would become their profile picture.

After that, they walked down the steps and went to join their daughters.

2016

Irfan heard the fireworks going and was rudely awakened. His shoulders were stiff, considering the awkward position he had nodded off in. He straightened up, grabbing the remote control and switching on the television. His wife must have turned it off and gone to bed.

Had they won? A flicker of hope ignited in him as he heard the celebrations. But he knew, it was from the wrong part of town. His wife came running into the lounge, dishevelled and in tears. She held her mobile phone to her ears and cried as she tried to talk to the person on the line.

Shit.

Irfan turned up the volume. He read the news ticker speeding across the screen. Brexit: Europe stunned by UK Leave vote.

Fuck.

Was this for real? He had stayed in front of the telly for most of the night, confident that the Remainers would win. He would win. He had dozed off, quite ready to celebrate in the morning.

He stared at his wife, who mouthed 'Ingrid'. Her Polish business partner and best friend. He ran his fingers through his hair and paced through the Twitter feeds. This was unreal. They were confident that it wasn't going to end this way. His brother called him, wanting to discuss the situation. But he didn't want to. Listening to his brother's voice made him suddenly long for home. He wished he was back in the dusty clamour of Agra. Where Brexit wouldn't touch him. Where he wouldn't have to explain himself because he was different.

Then he shook his head in disbelief. Who was he kidding? He had been discriminated even there, in his 'home'. He remembered her scent. That promise of first love. And how there too, he had been told—go find your own people. Don't mess with our daughter.

His wife put the phone away and smiled at him. A trembling, watery kind of smile that told him she was sorry. Sorry for what was happening in their country. Her country. Would he ever feel that he belonged here now? He had to get ready for work. He felt the prickle of sweat on his brow line. He didn't want to face anyone at work. He didn't want their looks of pity, or commiseration. He didn't want to see the sickly smooth smiles of the Leavers. His wife came up to him and hugged him. He moved to stroke her on her head, but staring at her golden hair, he felt like he wasn't entitled to touch her. She was the other.

His city had voted to leave. When he walked out of his front door, he looked down the street. The terraced houses, displaying their English front gardens proudly. The street awash with the riotous colours of roses, pansies and dahlias. He stared at the bunting festooning the windows. His street, mostly remain. But he would have to leave this safe space and venture into the city centre. It had to be done, and once again he felt fear. Fear for the colour of his skin. Fear for his name.

He walked to his car, once again cursing the neighbour's son who always parked his bike too close. When would he ever learn, that kid? His eyes fell on the side of his blue Mercedes. Scratched on the surface, the words screamed out at him. *Go home.*

Irfan stared at it. Somehow it did not shock him. Nor scare him. Some idiotic teenagers must have done it for a laugh. A dare. He looked around. There was no one suspicious around. The old pensioner from three doors down went past on his mobility scooter, tipping his hat. The high school kids in their smart blazers and sneaky spliffs sauntered by. They brushed past him like he never existed. That too was normal. Irfan's temper rose. Now he'd have to get the car in the workshop and get it fixed. People would read the damn words. He'd have to pay to get this bloody thing fixed.

Go home, it said. This was home. He ran back into the house. Straight into the bathroom and turned on the tap. He splashed water on his face, and then, he covered his face with his hands. His body trembled as he sat down on the toilet and breathed hard. He wiped away the tears that came despite himself.

Someone had singled him out and told him to go home. He tried to reason with himself. This was the repercussion that was inevitable. They didn't mean it personally. It was a baggage he would have to carry all his life. He wiped his tears with the back of his hand. He had struggled to make this country his home. His wife was English. What if she, for even one second, regretted having married him?

Irfan sat back and waited for his breathing to become normal. He would not let himself down this time. Nor his family. This was his home, and he was going to stay. He heard the buzzing of a fly trapped in the bathroom. It flew around, smashing into the mirror and then drunkenly towards the window. Outside he heard television screaming out opinions. His wife knocked on the door, asking if he was okay. The fly escaped through the open window. Irfan stepped out of the bathroom. He would take the car to the garage after work. He splashed on his favourite aftershave and stepped out. He was ready.

Mango Season

My great-grandmother died at the age of a hundred and two. She had been pickling mangoes on the terrace on a muggy May afternoon. We found her with a piece of mango in her mouth and a satisfied smile wrinkling one cheek.

Boroma, was one hell of a woman. The terrace was a steep climb and she climbed it every day. She had outlived her husband and her son by decades and yet she had been optimistic and famous for her razor-sharp tongue. After my grandfather died, we moved to the ancestral home, a big cavernous house with surrounding gardens full of fruit trees. As a child, I loved to listen to her stories of the legends of each tree in the garden. They all seemed to have illustrious lives. My mother was relegated to become the kitchen helper, while Boroma still cooked and fed the family. It was difficult at first, my mother not adjusting to playing second fiddle to an eighty year-old woman, and my father having to listen to her moan all the time. But the situation was such, we couldn't afford to live in our flat any more, and Boroma refused to sell the house. But I profited from the deal, because this house had so much history and hiding places and secrets, that it made up for most of my free time at home.

After the last rites, I decided I would move into her room. It faced the east and the morning light would be perfect for painting. I think Boroma would have liked me to occupy her room. She doted on me more than anyone else in the family. The room had been cleaned and sanctified and I felt robbed of her presence. It no longer smelled of coconut hair oil and jasmine. I missed seeing her tiny body bent over her flower-laden gods and goddesses, her spider-web hands ringing the prayer-bell as she chanted her mantras.

I lay down on the four-poster bed and spread my arms. How many times I had slept here beside her, while she stroked my hair and told me stories of the past: of life during the Raj, the struggle for freedom and the climax of independence. She had been a freedom fighter who had marched alongside her husband, shouting slogans, sewing clothes, attending to the wounded along with other brave women.

But Boroma had been very western in her upbringing. Theirs had been an influential family, enough to make the British wary of them and keep them happy. She had learned to play the piano and sing arias. She had a Scottish nurse who taught her to wear a corset and write poetry. Her husband had studied law in England and was a highly regarded barrister. They led a lavish lifestyle until one day my great-grandfather crossed paths with Mahatma Gandhi and he was converted. He gave up all his English airs and joined the fight for independence.

I wonder what Boroma had to say about this ideology. Her meat-eating, ballroom-dancing husband suddenly became vegetarian, gave up his silks for linen and followed the Mahatma through the countryside. She resisted for some time, unable to sacrifice her piano and her Burns, but one day her husband came home to find a blaze of fire that he could see from miles away. She had set fire to her piano, her gowns and a library full of English literature. When he asked her why she had done this, she fell at his feet and asked for forgiveness: for loving the British more than her own kind. She then fought to oust them from her country.

I loved these stories. She told them as if they had happened just the other day. I'd make her describe her gowns and perfumes. I couldn't believe my Boroma in such finery. She would smile mischievously and say that she allowed a wayward dream where she would be in her taffeta dress and play the Moonlight Sonata. Why then did she renounce them? Surely she could have kept her piano? Boroma always smiled and said it was for the best.

One night, as I slept on this bed, I felt her bony fingers caress my cheek. She was singing softly. It was one of her favourite Burns' compositions.

Why, why tell thy lover
Bliss he never must enjoy?
Why, why undeceive him,
And give all his hopes the lie?
O why, while fancy, raptur'd slumbers,
Chloris, Chloris all the theme,
Why, why would'st thou, cruel-
Wake thy lover from his dream?

I waited till she finished her song. The moonlight was shining on her face and I saw that she was crying.

"Why are you sad, Boroma?" I asked her.

She continued to stroke my face. "You have his eyes, my lovely. Definitely his eyes. He had such beautiful eyes." She whispered and stared out into the darkness.

It was true. My grandfather, her only son, had had beautiful eyes: like the colour of the sea after sunset, a deep grey with diluted hints of gold that shone as the waves ebbed and flowed. Only if you looked deep into his eyes, could you see the golden sheen behind the grey.

He died when I was eight. His death was the only one Boroma took very badly. She would sit in her room and look at his photographs for hours: pictures of him as a child, cuddling in her arms and as a young man, in his air-force uniform. He was tall, well-built and with a good sense of humour. He was treated differently by everyone, as if someone regal. His colouring, his stature, his demeanour were fit for a king, everyone said. My father did not inherit his stature or his looks and that was a disappointment for Boroma. "Gone towards his mother's side of the family," she'd mutter, clicking her tongue.

Now I had those eyes. I was her first great-grand-child and the only one to have inherited her son's looks. My eyes, she told me, were an artist's delight and sorrow. The artist would delight in the challenge to paint such beauty and then break down in defeat. He would never be able to capture the essence and the magic held in them.

So I moved into her room, with my canvasses and paints. My mother decided to move the bed to her room as I needed more space for my work. It was dismantled and stacked on the floor. I looked at it guiltily. It had stayed in this room for 79 years. My great-grandparents' marital bed. The mahogany still gleamed. I ran my fingers along the silk-like finish. I felt the textures of the carvings. Smooth. So finely chiselled, my fingers glided across intricate rose patterns. As I caressed the wood, I felt something wedged between the wooden slats. Carefully, I prised it out.

It was an ivory-coloured leather glove. It looked frail and discoloured with age. The golden trim was moth eaten. I felt around the slats and found its pair. They looked like they had been cherished, not forgotten in the depths of this cavernous bed. Did they belong to my Boroma? Were these the only Western possessions that she saved from the fire? Something she held close to her and remembered her glorious days of being a 'memsahib'? I read the label inside. Made in England. They felt soft and powdery like butterfly wings. They crackled in my hands, and I discovered some bits of paper folded inside them.

I removed the papers to see if these gloves would fit me. The papers were thick and glossy. Unusual to stuff gloves with, I thought. I unfolded one, and just as I had expected, it was not stuffing at all. It was a thick letter-paper. The words were in neat copperplate, black ink that had faded to a purplish-brown tint.

You were an angel descending from heaven, when you walked down the stairs last night. I could only hold my breath and watch…and my lips held a prayer in your name. You are not real, my love, because I cannot touch you. I cannot feel the gossamer of your skin. You are a vision to me. Gliding in front of my eyes, but when I reach out to touch you, you flit away. My chest hurts in disappointment, and my arms hunger for a stolen embrace. How I burn when he takes you in his arms and whirls you around the room. But when I look in your eyes, I feel assurance. They are empty. They search the room frantically… and then they stop when they find me. That is all I want from you.

I stared at the note and wondered who it was addressed to. Why it was hidden in a glove in my great-grandmother's bed, I had no idea. I pulled out another piece of paper.

It is mango season again. I delight in the first bite of its sweet flesh. The fragrance stays with me all the time. Its juices burst into my mouth and tease my tongue so. The mango taunts me: of flavours forbidden to me. And you? Do you think a bottle of your pickle can satisfy my longing? Why must you punish me, and leave me to hunger for you in my mind? Come away with me. I'll give you my life.

John.

The raw sexuality of this letter washed over me, and my body prickled in response. Erotic visuals danced inside my head as I wondered who the dancers in this dreamscape were. John, an Englishman and …?

I searched for other letters in the bed, but couldn't find any more. My attention went back to the gloves. They looked so fragile and vulnerable on the smooth, hard wood. I held them close. They smelled musty and faintly of the mahogany bed. I pulled out all the bits of paper tightly rolled into each finger of the gloves. There were ten in all. I flattened them out and read them. I read and re-read them. The words made love to the paper. I surrendered myself to them.

By now I was beginning to see. This love-dance was being danced by my Boroma and John.

My dearest,

I know that you will not go against your husband, or your religion, or your country. The stars are against our union, but what is done is done, and no one can undo it now.

I prayed for you to come away with me. I am returning home to Devon next month. My passage has been confirmed on the S.S. Duchess. My time here is done, but yours is just beginning.

Everyone has left our cantonment and the district commissioner has said there is no more future for us here. There will be bloodshed, my beloved. My heart aches to think what lies ahead. It is a terrible thing that the people of this land must die in order to regain their freedom. And you, dear heart, I can see you marching alongside your brave husband… towards your freedom.

But my heart also rejoices in the freedom. You will have your identity and pride restored to its full glory. You will know happier times, my dear. I promise you. Accept my parting gift with love. And perhaps in another lifetime, we will be reunited again. In a different land, in happier times…

I will love you forever
Yours
Captain John Everett

I read every word until I could see the naked truth between the lines. The proof of what the letter seemed to suggest. Did Boroma burn her Englishness to mourn the loss of her true love or did she do it to remind herself of her reality? She had deceived my great-grandfather. She had marched with him, fighting for their freedom, fully knowing that she loved an Englishman. I found that I was shaking… but I had no name for my emotions.

I thought of my beloved Boroma. A fiery, outspoken woman. Her never-say-die attitude. Of course she would have had an affair with 'the enemy', if her heart led her to it. There was more to her than just taffeta gowns and ballroom waltzes. Or linen saris and hunger strikes. All the time, there was one secret burning inside her. Eighty odd years of secrecy. Of remembering and hurting. Yes, I was sure of that. That was her punishment. The price she paid for her secret.

I realised then, that night, when she had cried and stroked my face, she had been looking into my eyes and remembering. She had said I also had those eyes… those deep grey eyes flecked with gold, the eyes of her English lover, who had been lost to her forever.

Acknowledgements

My sincerest thanks to everyone who continues to support me on my writing journey. Thank you to my family for putting up with my quirks and supporting me unconditionally. To my friends and first readers – Romy Thomas, Bethany Rivers, John White. My excellent and supportive tutors at Cardiff University – Shelagh Weeks, John Freeman, Richard Gwyn and Bella Kemble. To Mrs Brendish, who started me on this journey in the first place – I was incredibly lucky to have her as my English teacher in school.

To Farhana Shaikh, for believing in me and for being such a star. For upholding the short story form and supporting diverse writers.

To Dahlia Publishing, for their technical and editorial support in bringing this collection together.

A big thank you to my writing group in Winchester, The Taverners: Claire Fuller, Amanda Oosthuizen, Louise Taylor, Isabel Rogers, Judith Heneghan, Richard Stillman, Rebecca Lyon, Paul Davies, Emma Scattergood, Jake Wallis Simons.

To Matthew West of ArtfulScribe for championing creativity in the Hampshire community. To Joanna Barnard, leading the SO:Write Women's Writing Workshops in Southampton. A couple of stories were born there.

To my sister, Ronjita, for being my first ever reader from age 5 possibly and continuing to stick with me! To my mother, Swati Das, and my mother-in-law, Kalpana Bhattacharya, for being super women.

And finally, a big thank you to Syamantak and my girls. For everything.

About the Author

Susmita Bhattacharya was born in Mumbai. Her short fiction has been widely published, been nominated for the Pushcart Prize and broadcast on BBC Radio 4. Her novel, *The Normal State of Mind*, was published in 2015 by Parthian (UK) and Bee Books (India). It was long listed for the Words to Screen Prize by the Mumbai Association of Moving Images (MAMI). She teaches contemporary fiction at Winchester University and also facilitates the Mayflower Young Writers workshops, a SO:Write project based in Southampton.

Website: https://susmitabhattacharya.com
Twitter:@susmitatweets